P9-DGG-114

Stick Boy

BOOKS BY JOAN T. ZEIER

The Elderberry Thicket

Stick Boy

Stick Boy

Joan T. Zeier

Atheneum   1993   *New York*

Maxwell Macmillan Canada
Toronto

Maxwell Macmillan International
New York   Oxford   Singapore   Sydney

ATHENEUM
Macmillan Publishing Company
866 Third Avenue
New York, NY 10022

MAXWELL MACMILLAN CANADA, INC.
1200 Eglinton Avenue East
Suite 200
Don Mills, Ontario M3C 3N1

Macmillan Publishing Company is part of the
Maxwell Communication Group of Companies.

Book design by Crowded House Design

First edition
Printed in the United States of America

10 9 8 7 6 5 4 3 2 1

Library of Congress Cataloging-in-Publication Data
Zeier, Joan T.
    Stick Boy / Joan T. Zeier.—1st ed.
        p.   cm.
    Summary: When a seven-inch growth spurt in the sixth grade
makes skinny, self-conscious Eric a school misfit and the victim of
the class bully, he is led to befriend Cynthia, a proud and
spirited black girl who is disabled.
    ISBN 0–689–31835–9
    [1. Schools—Fiction. 2. Popularity—Fiction. 3. Friendship—
Fiction. 4. Bullies—Fiction. 5. Afro-Americans—Fiction.
6. Physically handicapped—Fiction.] I. Title.
PZ7.Z3935St 1993
[Fic]—dc20   92–23326

To all my grandsons:
When you look for a leader, it could be *you*

Chapter 1

There was actually quite a nice pattern in the floor tile, Eric thought. Strange, he had never really noticed the gray and black geometrics before—not until now, on his way out. It was a noisy material. The click of his mother's heels and the scuff of his joggers echoed through the halls as they passed the doors of his former classrooms. Eric Bonner would soon be out of this school forever.

Good-bye, school. Good-bye, Miss Gray. For a second, the image of his teacher's calm face burst into his thoughts. Miss Gray had taught sixth grade for a long time. She understood. Eric felt a dangerous tingling in the corners of his eyes and fought the tears. Desperately, he focused his attention on the floor's hard surface. It looked like slate. Or possibly quarry tile.

He concentrated on the clicks and the scuffs of their footsteps until the heavy school door had closed behind them. As they walked toward the parking lot, he sneaked a look at his mother. She had really blown her cool in the principal's office, but now she was taking long, deep breaths in time with her steps. Mom had her own ways of coping.

After they got in the car, she sat frozen for a few seconds, clutching the steering wheel. Then she examined herself in the rearview mirror.

"Look at me," she sighed. "My mascara is smudged." She took out a tissue and poked it at the corner of her eye.

"I noticed it in the principal's office," said Eric. "I would have said something, but it didn't seem like the right moment."

His mother looked at him sharply and then relaxed a little. One of the small, manicured hands that had struck the principal's glass desk top so sharply a few minutes before reached toward Eric's face, lifted a wind-blown strand of his fine white-blond hair, and put it gently into place. She smiled sadly.

"Did I make a fool of myself in there?" she asked.

"Nah."

"You're not much help, you know."

"I didn't want you to make such a fuss, Mom. I coulda took it."

Her eyes flashed like blue diamonds. "I don't want to hear that, Eric," she said. "We're on our own, just the two of us. That's why we've got to be tough. We can't let people push us around. Right?"

Eric looked down, unable to answer. He wished he had worn his Quatre Cinq T-shirt for luck. Maybe that shirt was what he'd needed all along, when bad things were happening to him.

"Eric, Eric." Even though she didn't say it, he recognized her what-shall-I-do-with-you voice. She was quiet for a minute, as if regrouping her thoughts. Then she went on.

"You have to realize that it's not *you* who has the problem. Sprouting up seven inches in a year was not your choice, but it's who you are right now. Those kids who call you a freak are the ones with problems. Miss Gray knew that. She was right in telling me what was going on. You've got enough to deal with—your father walking out and all."

She never failed to bring that up. Eric knew that was one of the big differences between his mom and him. She couldn't stop talking about the things that hurt her, and for Eric it was just the opposite. He couldn't *start*.

His mother rested her forehead on the steering wheel.

"This whole situation is just unreal," she said. "You heard the principal and the counselor in there. They as much as denied there was any problem at all. 'Natural playground rivalry,' they called it. Can you blame me for jerking you out of school?"

Eric shrugged. He was starting to recover from that scene in the principal's office, and, now that he had a chance to think about it, being out of school for a while might be all right. Sixth grade was no big deal, anyway. He could probably learn just as much by hanging out at the library every day.

Maybe he'd have a chance to put on some weight so he wouldn't look like such a bean pole. He knew what he looked like—he wasn't blind, for Pete's sake. Who'd want a friend who towered above them, long, skinny arms and legs always getting tangled up, and that same little-kid face he'd had since kindergarten?

"Well, it's all over now," he said agreeably.

His mother straightened up, reading his mind. "What do you mean, 'It's all over'?" she snapped. "There just happens to be a law about that. What we have to do now is find you a new school. And I really can't afford to sit here wasting time." She turned the key in the ignition.

It wasn't what they wanted, but it was all they could get. The schools Mrs. Bonner wanted were full.

Eric felt a sense of relief. At least this school was small. He had seen it briefly in their hasty afternoon of searching. A weatherworn round sign, THE LIGHT OF

LIFE EDUCATION CENTER, hung between two rusty posts. There was honesty in the cracked sidewalk and faded paint. No false fronts, that was for sure.

His mother had scared him half to death talking about schools with "innovative concepts," whatever those were. Like the "school without walls." The thought of vast, open spaces with nothing to hide behind made Eric's flesh quiver inside his shirt. LIGHT OF LIFE would do just fine.

The November wind grabbed at Eric's upturned collar the next morning as he followed his mother, who had stopped to register him on her way to work. Once inside, the process was hasty. The principal shoved papers at them, explaining that she was substituting for a sick teacher that day and had to hurry to her classroom soon. Still, her eyes were warm and her voice sounded sincere enough.

"I wish I had more time to spend with you," she said apologetically. "Basically, we want our students to learn moral and ethical values along with the academics. Unlike some private schools, we recruit minority students. And, as Christians, we offer a Bible class once a week. Optional."

Eric watched his mother's face, but it didn't show any reaction at all. That surprised him a little. Grandma and Grandpa Bonner were regular churchgoers, and his dad, too. But that was back in Minnesota. His mom had finally won full custody and moved away, and they had never gone near a church since. It was one of the things he missed.

"The sixth-grade room is on the second floor," said the principal. "I'll take you up to meet Miss Arthur."

Eric could taste the orange juice he'd had for breakfast. He hoped he wasn't going to be sick.

"Don't trip on your shoestrings," his mother cautioned, pushing him ahead of her. "I do wish you would tie them."

The stairs were narrow, with metal strips edging the badly worn green linoleum. No quarry tile here. He clumped along silently behind the principal, wishing he were someplace else. At least at his old school he had known what to expect.

"This is Miss Arthur's room. Miss Arthur, come and meet Mrs. Bonner and Eric."

Miss Arthur's brown curls cascaded to the shoulders of her light blue cardigan, and her voice was like rose petals when she spoke to Eric's mother. When it was his turn, her blue eyes welcomed him, but he quickly mumbled hello and stepped back. Miss Arthur seemed too young and pretty to be a teacher.

"I have to get to work, Eric," said his mother. "You know which bus to catch to get home?"

He nodded, accepting her anxious smile. He felt a touch of panic when she turned to leave, but then he remembered his Quatre Cinq T-shirt. Under his gray-striped button-down, he wore it like a fetish: black knit lettered in silver, an iridescent Q glowing at each end. Before leaving his room this morning, Eric had stared at the Quatre Cinq poster on his wall. He had tried to tap into the joy and self-confidence that shone from the rock singer's handsome dark-skinned face. Eric had memorized most of the songs. Right now, "That Sinking Feeling" was running through his head.

"This morning we begin with math and science," Miss Arthur was saying, "so I'll give you those books now. Do you mind sitting in the back? Otherwise, I could rearrange—"

"In back is fine." Eric was almost startled at his own loud voice. But he knew enough to speak up when he really wanted something, and a backseat was definitely the safest.

He watched his shoes lead him to the back of the room. They measured out squares of gray linoleum, with flecks that must have once been colored. He smelled wax and paste and stale air. Thank God he was early. Even so, he could feel people staring at him as he walked.

"That sinking feeling / turning upside down / walking on my hands / into Spidertown . . ." Eric tucked his thumb across the palm of his right hand and spread the fingers of his left hand wide around the books he carried. It was Quatre Cinq's sign: four and five.

The first time he had heard one of the songs on the radio, it had been like a voice talking directly to him. Quatre Cinq's voice could crest and fall and scrape blackboards, but beneath it all was a calm, velvet reassurance—like a thick cushion that could break your plunge out of a nightmare. Later, Eric had learned that the singer's name was French for "four five" and that he claimed those two numbers had magical power.

Eric slid into his seat, keeping his eyes on the desk top. Old but nice. Golden oak wood. Too bad about the ugly gouges—some dumbbell's initials. He arranged the math and science books in front of him. Red for math and green for science. Same as at his old school, only shabbier.

Sensing movement at the front of the room, Eric looked cautiously through his pale eyelashes, without raising his chin. A short black girl entered the room clumsily, steadying herself with an aluminum cane. Close behind, carrying books, was a lady, probably her mother. She helped the girl adjust her leg braces and get settled at her desk up front. She leaned to kiss her, but the girl turned her head away quickly, as though embarrassed.

Eric stared at his desk again. He didn't even look up when the sound of heavy boots jarred the floor two rows over.

"Hey, Jer, did you catch 'Precinct 40' last night?" This was a boy's voice, older-sounding, domineering.

Eric recognized it at once. It was the kind of voice he had heard in other classrooms. *Beware*, it told him.

"Yeah, cool." Jer's voice was quiet. Eager to please. "How about you, Tyler?"

"Of course, man. How about that scene where they got the guy in the locker room—"

A bell rang, and the last-minute swell of students scurried toward their desks.

"All rise for the Pledge of Allegiance. . . ."

He hadn't heard that for a while, had almost forgotten how it went. Eric moved his lips while the others recited.

When they had finished, Miss Arthur smiled. "Class, we have a new student. Eric Bonner." Still smiling, she fluttered a gentle arm in his direction. Every head in the room turned toward him. Curious eyes devoured his slight, light features as if they were pancakes and syrup. He heard a few polite "Hi, Eric"s before they decided he was only oatmeal and lost interest.

A large wall chart diagrammed the classroom seating, and Miss Arthur printed his name in bold letters in Seat *Five,* Row *Four.* He felt his spine tingle. Could this really be a coincidence?

Automatically, Eric matched up names, counting syllables. His own name had four syllables, so he needed to match up with five-syllable people. Tyler Wayne, the boy whose voice had put Eric's defense system on alert—

three syllables. No surprise there. Funny, the boy called Jer was really Jeremiah Peel—a five. Could be a possibility. And the girl with leg braces was also a five—Cynthia Jebber.

Right off, he could count her out as a likely friend. Not that he had anything against girls, but the kind of friend he needed right now would have to be a guy. Well, he couldn't expect the four-five formula to work out *every* time.

Math class was pretty interesting, the way Miss Arthur taught it. Eric had always liked math, but it was amazing how some teachers could take all the fun out of it. Chalk up a point for Miss Arthur. She acted as though she enjoyed every minute of it and then headed into reading, mercifully asking nothing of Eric. His eyes were on the clock. Sooner or later there would be recess. That was when trouble usually started.

He sneaked another look at Tyler Wayne, hoping that his first impression had been wrong. Tyler was more mature than most of the boys: almost as tall as Eric but filled out, strong and well-built. Probably the girls thought he was good-looking, although something about him reminded Eric of an ape. Maybe it was the hint of a smirk that never seemed to leave his face.

" 'On the fourth try,' " read Miss Arthur, " 'his rope slipped and he felt his footing give way. Frantically, he clawed for another hold.' " She looked up from her book, and her eyes were serious.

"What thoughts do you think came to Edgar's mind?" she asked. "How would *you* feel on the edge of a precipice?"

A girl in a plaid dress raised her hand. "I'd be really scared," she said.

Miss Arthur nodded. "Yes, I think we all would, Peggy. Francine, how about you?"

Francine was two rows ahead of Eric and two rows over. He could see her fine-chiseled profile and her serious face, framed by long dark hair. "I might wish I had a second chance—to make up for mistakes I've made."

"Very good, Francine." Miss Arthur looked pleased. This must be the morals-and-ethics training. "Anyone else?"

"It seems to me"—Cynthia Jebber's voice carried to the back of the room with a crisp edge—"it was the perfect time for instant religion."

Miss Arthur hugged the book close to the nicely shaped front of her blue cardigan and smiled a bit uncertainly. The bell rang for recess.

Chapter 2

Eric forced himself to follow the others out of the class-room. Whatever happens in the next twenty minutes could make or break the entire rest of my life, he thought. He put on his jacket, and inside the pockets his hands formed a desperate four-five sign. Then he sneaked a glance to see if there was someone else who seemed to be alone. But not a girl. Hanging around with a girl was not a smart move.

Tyler Wayne had crashed on ahead, to be the first one out, and the short boy named Jeremiah was left behind. His eyes met Eric's. They were brownish, fright-ened, like a deer's. Eric half smiled—his lips turned just far enough so he could straighten them quickly if necessary.

"Do you want to play tetherball with us?" someone asked in Eric's left ear. A girl, of course.

"I'm Peggy Di Angelo," she said. She was the girl in the plaid dress. She had tangled blond hair and long front teeth. Beside her was the pretty, serious one. Only now she was smiling.

"Hi. I'm Francine Topp," she said.

"Uh . . . sure," muttered Eric. He looked back toward the spot where Jeremiah had been, but he had disappeared. All the other boys seemed to have melted into a noisy group that was already halfway down the stairs.

The only ones who remained in the classroom were the teacher and Cynthia, the girl with the leg braces.

Peggy and Francine were chattering away and he tried to hear what they were saying, but they talked too fast. He couldn't listen to them and think ahead about the right thing to do. Whatever it was he had done wrong at the other school, this time he had to do it right.

When the three of them got outside, he saw that the boys had gathered on the side of the playground opposite the tetherball.

He turned to Francine. "I guess I'll go with the other guys," he said.

"Okay. We'll see you later," she said cheerfully. She did not look offended.

He walked toward the group of boys. They were in

a half-circle around Tyler Wayne. They were all looking down at the bare dirt beyond the edge of the blacktop.

"Look like anyone we know?" Tyler asked loudly. He had a long box-elder branch in his hand, and jabbed it into the spot they were eyeing. Then his chin jerked up and he stared steadily as Eric approached.

"Hi, new kid," he said, but there was no welcome in his voice. "Hey, don't feel left out. Come over and see the good picture I drew."

Eric pushed up the collar of his jacket and kept walking slowly. Walking into the trap, he thought. Just like before. He could hear them breathing; a few muffled snickers roared like oceans in his ears. They waited for him, and when he reached them, Tyler Wayne jabbed the stick at the ground again.

"Aren't I a good artist?" He grinned, and they all laughed.

Eric looked, and for a second felt relief. He had expected to see a dirty picture scrawled in the dirt. This was nothing but a stick figure. Just a tiny, round head above the long, straight body, and lines for arms and legs. Then his heart sank as he realized that Tyler had already zeroed in on the one thing about himself he could never hide: his superspindly body.

"Got it just about right, I guess," said Tyler, and mimicked the stiff-jointed stance of his creation. Some of the boys nearly fell down laughing, and others held it to a smirk; but they were all looking at him, Eric.

Quatre Cinq would have strolled right up to the stick figure, toe-to-toe, and mimicked it, just like Tyler. "Sure enough, it's just like we were born twins," he would say; and even though they still laughed, they would know he was one of them. But Eric couldn't do it. He stood mute, glued to the ground, feeling humiliated, just as he always did. His face was marked with hurt and disappointment for everyone to see, until, at an unheard signal, the group turned away and ignored him.

"We've got this dog, man," one of them said. "She's having pups any day now. Purebred German shorthairs. You know how much we're gonna get for them?"

"How much?" somebody asked.

"More than two hundred dollars each," boasted the first boy. "And she'll most likely have ten or twelve pups."

"Wow!" At least a few of the boys looked impressed.

"How much did you have to pay for that dog?" asked Tyler Wayne.

"She woulda been two hundred dollars—same as these pups. Only we got her from my uncle. He gave her to us cheap."

"How about giving me a deal, Johnson? I'm your best friend, and I'd sure like a dog like that."

"My dad's the one to talk to, and he don't give deals. Sorry, Tyler. Anyway, I thought you had a dog."

"Sure, but he's just a mutt. Can't make any money with him." Tyler turned toward Eric again, his question swerving like a runaway truck. "How about you, Stick Boy? You got a dog?"

Eric swallowed hard. "No." His voice came out small and squeaky. "Pets aren't allowed in our building."

"Oh-ho-ho-ho!" Tyler threw up his hands. "Did you hear that, guys? Stick Boy says pets aren't allowed in his building. What a shame! I'll bet the real reason is, his mama is afraid a doggy might knock down her puny little Stick Boy."

Speak up now. Don't let him get away with that name.

"My right name is *Eric*." Somehow he squeaked out the words.

As though he had not even heard, Tyler turned away and loudly snuffled some imaginary phlegm.

"I'll bet even Jerry Peel's got a dog," he said. "How about that, Peel—you got a dog?"

The deer eyes were as wary as if it were third day of open season, but Eric noticed how the shoulders of Jeremiah's shabby jean jacket stiffened, as if he were bracing himself.

"Sure. I've got a German shepherd. Nobody messes with our family, I can tell you," he said. Maybe Jeremiah was tougher than he looked.

The other boys chimed in, boasting about their own pets; and for the rest of recess, Eric stood back, unnoticed.

When the bell rang, Eric ended up among the girls again. Several of them were ahead of him on the stairs, half whispering but loud enough for him to hear.

"That Cynthia must have a special excuse to stay in at recess."

"What's the matter with her anyway? Did she have an accident?"

One smart, important-sounding voice: "No. It's some kind of birth defect. She's partly paralyzed. She has to wear diapers and everything."

"Oh my gosh! Really?"

"Pee-yew! How awful." That was Francine Topp's voice.

"My mother said we should be nice to her."

"But *diapers*? What about the lunchroom?"

"Yuk! Eating near her would gross me out!"

Eric winced. They were talking about the girl with leg braces. She must be new, too. Well, too bad for Cynthia. Anyway, it looked as if he wouldn't be the only one without friends in this school.

He heard a commotion behind him, and everyone moved over to let Tyler Wayne and his friends through. Tyler came lunging up, two steps at a time, catching Eric's shoulder, throwing him against the wall.

Tyler looked back with a toothy grimace. "Ha, Stick Boy!" he snickered, just loud enough for everyone to hear.

Chapter 3

Eric had survived Light of Life for more than two weeks now, but nothing had improved. Tyler Wayne was waiting with a new gibe at every opportunity. It was amazing how much stuff went on right under Miss Arthur's slightly upturned nose. All the while she went on smiling, probably thinking about what a good teacher she was.

It was no wonder that the best part of every day was the bus ride home. Eric was the only kid on the bus going to an older part of the city, and it took a half hour to get there.

By the time he got on the bus each afternoon, it was a relief to lean his head against the window as the bus rolled along Victoria Avenue and to admire the rows of old-fashioned houses rimmed with balconies and cupolas. He had chosen a favorite and sometimes pretended that he lived there—part of a big, laughing, happy family.

Of course, three days a week there was no chance to daydream. Those were AMOS days—days when a noisy group called Artists and Musicians Over Sixty who lived in the Victoria Avenue area rode the bus on their way home from the senior center. They made the school lunchroom seem sedate. At first Eric had tried to sneak past them to the back of the bus, but it's not too easy to sneak when you're five feet eight and carrying a backpack.

They would always interrupt their camaraderie to find an empty seat for him. And after the first few times, the seat always seemed to be next to the same person— a slim man with a neatly trimmed white mustache and attentive gray eyes.

"So how's life treating you today, son?" he would ask, and it didn't matter what Eric answered, or even if he answered at all. The man nodded and looked sympathetic. And he was a great talker, always rambling on about something.

"Look at that. I see they're remodeling the old Ulysses Grant School—making an office building out of it, I hear. My father went to school there, before the turn of the century. In fact, he was named for President Grant—Grant Robinson, his name was—and he gave

me the same name. I never attended that school, though. How about you? What school do you go to?"

"Light of Life."

"Oh, sure. That's a private school, so that's why you ride this bus. I see. Pretty good school, is it?"

"Yes."

"Your mom and dad religious people?"

"My dad is, I guess."

And before Eric realized it, this Mr. Robinson knew all about him. Well, not everything. He would never want Mr. Robinson to know how he always got picked on, or how lonesome it got without a friend his own age.

"I'm a believer myself—always go to church on Sunday," Mr. Robinson went on. "The Lord gave me a better life than I deserved. Had a fine wife and two good kids. 'Course she's been gone now for three years, and my kids are clear across the country; but I'm still better off than some."

He gestured toward the other bus riders. "I've made a lot of friends through this AMOS group. We dance and share hobbies. I play in a little orchestra and have a real good time."

It must be nice, Eric thought. Maybe I need a group for Artists and Musicians Under Thirteen. Not that he was much of a musician. He had taken piano lessons back in Minnesota, but they couldn't afford that now.

He could write song lyrics, though. Lately, he had been trying some five-syllable, four-line verses, like those in Quatre Cinq's songs. When he got enough of them, he might send them to Quatre Cinq, in care of the record company.

On Tuesdays and Thursdays, without the AMOSs, the bus was very quiet. Then, like today, Eric had a seat all to himself and stared out at the old houses, noticing the intricate shingle patterns and the lacy cutouts in the gables. Studying details was another of Eric's hobbies. It was something he could do alone. He especially liked Mr. Robinson's house. It had a turret, with windows under the cone-shaped roof. It looked like a cozy place to write poems.

His own apartment building was much newer, but he wondered why nobody had bothered to make it beautiful. It was flat and plain, exactly like the two next to it. The bricks all matched so perfectly that they hardly looked real. Each building had identical evergreens framing the front door.

Leaning his head against the bus window, Eric drifted off into a fantasy. . . .

He imagined going inside the building next door, exactly like his own. Following the dull orange carpeting up the staircase to the third floor, he would turn to the right. He would insert his key; and the lock, being the same, would open, letting him into an apartment with the same few pieces of shabby furniture as his own. He would sit down to watch television, and two hours later the door would open and his mother, relaxed and smiling, would walk in and say:

"Eric! Guess what! My boss came in today and said I've been doing such a great job I deserve a bonus. He handed me a hundred-dollar bill, and that much will be added to my weekly paycheck from now on. Isn't that wonderful? To celebrate, I stopped in at the Chinese place and brought home a carryout of your favorite—cashew chicken."

He would run to her and hug her, smelling the flowery, clean LeJardin cologne she loved so much. Together they'd set the table.

"Now, tell me, Eric, how was your day?" Her voice would be light and gentle. "This is your third week at Light of Life. Are you happy there?"

"It's really great, Mom. The kids are so friendly—it seems like I fit right in. My best friends are Jeremiah and Francine, but the others are great, too. Tyler Wayne always has a good word for everyone, and a girl named Cynthia Jebber writes poetry, just like me. She has a weird sense of humor, too, and nobody even notices her disability."

"I'm so glad for you, Eric. Tell me more about it."

"Today Miss Arthur asked us if we'd like to participate

in something special these last two weeks before Christ-mas. Of course, everyone said yes. So we drew names. During the next two weeks, we'll be a Secret Friend to the person whose name we drew. Then the last day before Christmas vacation, at our party, we'll let them know who we are."

"That sounds like a wonderful idea, Eric. I can see that the school is teaching its students to care for others."

"You're right, Mom. This is all new to me, but I can tell it really works. I drew Cynthia Jebber's name, and Tyler Wayne accidentally saw it. Later he quietly asked me if I'd exchange with him, since he particularly likes doing nice things for Cynthia. But I told him I couldn't—I felt really lucky to have drawn her name in the first place. . . ."

The bus turned a sharp corner, throwing Eric against the side, bringing him back to reality. He saw that his stop was next and pushed the buzzer.

As he walked slowly toward the three identical apartment buildings, he could not help taking a quick look at the third-floor window next door where he had imagined himself to be.

The draperies were open, and it did not look at all like his place.

He followed the stained orange stair carpeting in his own building to the third floor, turned to the right, and unlocked the door. It was plain and shabby, just as they had left it.

He put away the box of cornflakes and carried the breakfast dishes to the sink. He was careful to use just one squirt of detergent, as his mother had instructed him, and ran a little warm water—no more than necessary. After washing and drying the dishes, he swept the scuffed linoleum. Then he pulled up a kitchen chair in front of the television.

Some days he could lose himself watching reruns. Today he couldn't. He kept thinking about his teacher: bubbly, optimistic Miss Arthur. She was really good at teaching all the subjects, but she sure had a lot to learn about kids. At times it seemed that she must have come from a different planet.

Like this afternoon, when she had asked the class to participate in the Secret Friend project. Hadn't she seen the doubting looks that crisscrossed the room? How could she push something like this on to a bunch of kids? Didn't she know that in sixth grade it isn't cool to be nice?

Her blue eyes had sparkled as she passed through the aisles with the empty paste jar containing all the slips with their names. When she came to his desk, Eric had avoided eye contact. Without enthusiasm, his thin hand reached in. In a single movement he unfolded, reclosed, and stuffed the slip into his pocket.

His mouth felt dry, and he licked his lips. He had known he could never be so lucky as to pick Francine's name. That would be asking too much. But why did it have to be Cynthia Jebber's? What could one misfit do for another? This wasn't going to help either one of them.

Eric wasn't the only one who was disappointed. As soon as the drawing began, so did the muffled groans. Tyler Wayne was carrying on as though in pain. He was used to having his own way, and this time his luck must have run out.

"I'm not gonna do it," he grumbled loudly, pounding his desk with his fist. "It's dumb, anyhow."

"It may not be easy," said Miss Arthur. "But I have confidence that you boys and girls can make this a rewarding experience."

Dream on, Miss Arthur, dream on. . . .

Eric switched the TV channel, wishing that by some magic a music video would appear. No such luck, though. The music videos were all on cable, and his mother said they couldn't afford cable. The only way he ever got to see them was by hanging around stores where they sold TVs. One day he had been lucky enough to catch Quatre Cinq. Quatre Cinq, the great—the fantastic!

It had been "Yellow Brick Mode," a takeoff on *The Wizard of Oz*, with Quatre Cinq's big feet stuffed into these little ruby slippers. "Dancing in quicksand / takes real expertise. / Don't try it unless / you have shoes like these. / Cancel your tickets / a day in advance. / No ruby slippers? / Don't come to this dance. / Because I love you / don't want to lose you. / Ask my assistance. / I won't refuse you. . . ."

That was the thing about Quatre Cinq's music. He could make you believe that any day now you'd be able to rock right out of your bottomless pit and hit the stars. Yeah, any day now. With a sigh, Eric slumped in his chair and watched reruns until his mother got home.

Mrs. Bonner looked pale, and a lot of little wisps of hair had escaped from her hairdo. She dropped her purse on a chair as though it had a brick in it.

"You tired?" asked Eric.

She nodded, scarcely looking at him.

"What a creep," she said.

"Your boss?"

"Who else? If I had any choice, I'd be out of there so fast . . ."

"You could get another job. You're a good secretary."

"Never good enough to suit old Waldo. But the pay is better than I could get anywhere else, and I've got a family to support."

Eric winced. A family to support. That meant *him*. If only he could think of some way to make her happier.

Maybe he could run away. But he dismissed that stupid idea in a second. He knew well enough how his mom felt about him. He was the only one she had left. All she needed was for another guy to walk out of her life. He turned off the television and helped her start dinner.

Chapter 4

It was almost sickening to watch Francine and Peggy the next morning, acting like Miss Arthur's Secret Friend idea was the deal of the century.

"It's so neat!" Francine exclaimed. "I've got dozens of plans already."

"Me, too," Peggy agreed. "I love secrets. It'll be fun."

Another girl shook her head doubtfully. "I'm not so sure," she said. "If I start doing nice things, won't that person be sure to know?"

"The best way to keep people guessing is to do kind things for *everyone*," Miss Arthur suggested. Her face was already lit up like a Christmas tree.

"Hey, *I* do that all the time," Tyler Wayne said,

conning her with wide puppy-dog eyes and an angelic smile. It was amazing how careful he was to impress Miss Arthur. "Aren't I always your best helper?"

Eric slouched down in his seat at the back of the room, trying to be invisible. This was never going to work, he felt sure of that. It might work in that perfect world Miss Arthur came from, but not here in this classroom.

Look at Cynthia. From hearing her answer Miss Arthur's questions, he knew she was smart. More than smart, she was *sharp*. Even Francine's answers sounded like parrot-talk compared to Cynthia's. He wished he had the courage to start a conversation with her, but he wouldn't dare. Doing a thing like that would be sure to furnish Tyler Wayne with a new reason to ridicule both of them.

One day in reading group Miss Arthur had complimented Cynthia on a poem she wrote. That was the only time Eric had seen Cynthia smile. Her chin dropped its defiant thrust, and her whole face lit up. She had been pretty for a minute. But most of the time, with everyone ignoring her, she had nothing to smile about.

When the bell rang for recess, Eric took plenty of time getting his jacket and zipping it up. It was getting colder every day and had already snowed a little. His mother had bought him a new gray jacket. He had picked out a puffy quilted one, because it made him look fat.

The best thing about cold weather was that nobody liked to stand around. That was when most of the bad stuff happened—while they were standing around. A parent had volunteered for playground duty and tried to keep some active games going. So in spite of some of the kids complaining about "baby games," lately they had been playing wheel ball.

Everyone would run around the perimeter of a big circle while the person in the middle, who was "it," tried to hit one of the runners, who would then take his or her place in the center. The game had already started when Eric joined it, but he managed to slip in without calling attention to himself.

He kept alert every second. His long legs could skip out of the way quickly if his brain gave them enough notice. Some slower kids got tagged a lot and had to be "it." But many of them had strong throwing arms and immediately tagged someone else. Eric did not want it to be him. He dashed, slowed, and dodged, always trying to anticipate the thrower's aim.

Then Tyler Wayne had the ball, and everyone danced for safety. Tyler's throwing was fast and accurate. His eyes roved among the players, choosing a victim. Everyone jostled to avoid him, and for a second, Eric was distracted by two girls who had cut suddenly in front of him.

Pow! The ball struck him hard on the shoulder, nearly knocking him off his feet. Luckily, his new coat had softened the blow.

"You're 'it,' Stick Boy," Tyler shouted, already far from the center.

Keep cool, Eric told himself, picking up the ball. Don't panic or you'll blow it for sure.

He looked for an easy target, but when he saw one, he held back. Hitting a weak boy or a nonathletic girl wouldn't prove anything. He aimed for Richard Johnson, the boy with the German shorthairs. The ball left his hand and went sailing, but Richard Johnson saw it coming. It bobbled to the ground. Eric ran to scoop it up, but he was tense. He knew he looked awkward.

Again he took aim. This time Jeremiah Peel was within range as he threw. Jeremiah was fast on his feet, too, and got out of the way. But somehow, there was Francine—in the wrong place at the wrong time. The ball struck her just above the knees.

"Oh no! You got me!" she squealed happily. She snatched up the ball and ran to the center, her rosy face prettier than ever. For her it was fun—just a game to be played and then forgotten. No consequences.

In spite of being good at sports, it took Francine three tries before she hit someone. Eric managed not to get tagged again for the rest of recess.

The bell rang. End of the round, Eric thought. He was as relieved as a fighter on the ropes.

As he walked toward the door, he heard a loud voice behind him. "Hey, Stick Boy! I like your new coat." It was Tyler Wayne.

Eric turned his head and sort of nodded, sure that Tyler was up to something.

"You look so puffy on top," continued Tyler slowly, as though searching for a new idea. "Puffy on top—with those long, skinny legs underneath . . . a stork! That's what you look like. A stork. Maybe we should call you *Stork* Boy."

Tyler's friends rewarded him with a big laugh.

"You're the one who can't shut his own beak, Tyler," snapped Peggy Di Angelo, who was nearby. This time the laugh was on Tyler, but it bounced off him like a Ping-Pong ball.

By the time they were hanging up their coats, Tyler had thought up another zinger. Half whispering so Miss Arthur wouldn't hear, he leaned toward Eric.

"How many babies did you deliver today?"

That was a good one, and plenty of people heard it. They were still trying to smother their giggles as Eric walked back to his desk.

At noon he pretended to be finishing some math problems, until everyone else had gone to the lunchroom. He figured on killing some time so he wouldn't be on the playground so long.

When he got to the lunchroom, he saw that he wasn't

so smart after all. All the tables were filled except for the one where Cynthia Jebber sat. There were empty chairs all around her. No place else to sit.

Eric headed for the farthest one. As he started to pull out the chair, the girl next to it put out her hand.

"Sorry, this one's saved," she said, tossing a sweater over it.

"For who?" he wanted to say, but he didn't dare. What if she answered, "Anyone but *you*"?

He had no choice. He put down his lunch bag directly across from Cynthia, and slid into the chair as quietly as possible. Cynthia didn't appear to notice him. She was very busy, her slim, dark fingers efficiently removing an orange peel.

Eric recalled the talk about Cynthia's diapers and took a silent whiff. All he could smell was her orange.

Even so, he kept his head down as he started his sandwich. What if they both looked up at the same time and their eyes met? He knew she must be sitting there, listening to him chew and thinking what a creep he was because he'd tried to sit far away from her.

So what's the big deal? he asked himself. What are you afraid of? The peanut butter caught in his throat and he started choking. When he jerked his head up and covered his mouth, Cynthia was staring at him.

"I know the Heimlich maneuver," she said coolly, and nibbled a section of orange.

" 'Scuse me," Eric muttered, recovering himself. "I'm okay now." He lifted his milk carton and took a sip. She was still looking at him.

He could feel a flush spreading across his cheeks. Why didn't she look at something else? She looked as though she were waiting for him to say something. What was there to say?

"Do you like staying up here at recess time?" he asked.

Cynthia made a funny little noise, like a snort. "Incredible that you should ask," she said.

Eric already knew that. As soon as the words left his mouth, he had known it was a stupid thing to say.

"I don't know what I meant." He tried to laugh, make it light, but that didn't work, either. His manners were as awkward as his body.

"Well, as a matter of fact," Cynthia said slowly, "it's not too bad, staying in. I make it a practice to concentrate on what I do well, not on what I can't do. I doubt that my success in life will depend on *recess*. Anyway, it's sure not worth climbing up and down those stairs for."

"How come you picked a school with stairs—or am I being too nosy?"

"Would you believe I got a scholarship?" With a chuckle, Cynthia gulped down her last orange slice. "Mm-hmm. The Harbor Street A.M.E. Church awarded me a full year's scholarship to this lovely private school. You wouldn't expect me to turn down an opportunity like that, would you?"

Eric didn't know what to say. Her words seemed sarcastic, but she said them in such a soft, humorous way that he couldn't be sure.

"I'm sure you deserved it," he said.

"You're right. I was a very bad girl last year and made fun of the minister. I did deserve it." This time he had no doubt that she was putting him on. Her brown eyes twinkled and a wide grin spread across her face.

"Now tell me the story of *your* life," she said.

Eric grinned, too, and took a big bite of his apple. For the first time since he'd come to school at Light of Life, he began to relax. He really liked this Cynthia. She might even be a Quatre Cinq fan. He decided to ask her.

"Do you—," he began, and then stopped suddenly. Jeremiah Peel had finished his lunch and was walking between the rows of tables, looking straight at Eric. There was a strange look on Jeremiah's face. What might he be thinking, seeing Eric laughing and talking with this weird Cynthia Jebber?

Eric looked down, studying the red and white textures of his apple until Jeremiah went out the door.

"My life story is junk," he mumbled. "Gotta go." He crumpled his milk carton and brown bag, pushed his chair away from the table, and, taking the apple with him, left the lunchroom in the direction Jeremiah Peel had gone.

Jeremiah was all alone on the playground, dribbling a basketball, zigzagging his way to the single rusty hoop down at the end.

Eric's long legs went into action; and by the time Jeremiah's ball hit the rim, Eric was there to grab the rebound. He bounced it a couple of times and then made an easy lay-up.

"You going out for one of the Y teams?" Jeremiah asked.

Eric let him have the ball. "I didn't know they had any," he said. "Can anybody join?"

"Sure. A lot of the guys are signing up. Jeez, we don't even have a decent gym at this school. How else are we supposed to learn?"

"I guess so."

"You'd be real good," Jeremiah said, looking him straight in the eyes. "You've got the height. I wish *I* was taller."

Eric hastened to return the compliment. "You're really fast on your feet, though." His heart was pounding. Talking like this was like the old days in Minnesota—back when he had just been one of the boys. If only he could make it last.

"Where do you go to sign up?" he asked.

"The principal had some blanks. You could probably get one yet. They start practicing during winter break."

"I think maybe I will. Thanks, Jeremiah."

"Hey, Jer!" Tyler Wayne's voice was loud and demanding, coming from the cement platform near the door. "Jerry Peel, come on over and look at my new watch!"

Jeremiah jerked around, startled, as though he'd been caught stealing. Without another glance at Eric, he dribbled the ball across the playground to Tyler's side. A minute later, the two of them were huddled together, all buddy-buddy, examining something under Tyler's pushed-up sleeve.

Eric was left standing empty-handed under the basket, without even a ball to masquerade his loneliness.

Chapter 5

Another week passed, but it seemed twice as long to Eric. When he thought about it, he must have been crazy that day, taking the kind of chances he had—trying to get friendly with people. He had probably done it because Jeremiah's small square face, with its sprinkling of light freckles, had, for some screwy reason, fit perfectly into the frame Eric carried around in his mind. Portrait of a best friend. Somebody he could trust. And for such a short kid, Jeremiah looked as if he could take care of himself.

Well, sometimes appearances are deceiving. It didn't seem to bother Jeremiah at all that he had dropped Eric like a hot potato the minute Tyler Wayne came around looking for a bootlicker. If that was his way of taking care of himself, it sure bashed Eric's ideas of "trust."

And as for Cynthia, she was even harder to figure out. That day at lunch she had been so ready to talk, and she made him almost forget that the two of them were anything but a couple of normal kids. Yet the next time he passed her desk and paused for a second, waiting for her to look up, she had deliberately kept her nose down in her book. Since then, she had turned her head the other way every time they happened to meet.

Either something was really bugging her, or she was just a moody person who didn't really want friends, anyhow. If somebody had done something rotten to her, Eric hadn't seen it happen. Except for holding his nose sometimes behind her back, even Tyler Wayne never did anything bad to her. Nobody did. In fact, nobody ever said anything to her at all.

He decided it was better not to try again. He tiptoed through the mine field of Tyler's stork jokes and wore his tan shirt a lot, hoping that he'd blend in and nobody would notice he was sitting at that oak desk. Like a prayer, he recited one of Quatre Cinq's lines over and over: "Keep travelin', man / till you find your niche." If only he could be sure there really *was* a niche for him. The traveling was the hard part.

Miss Arthur was giving Secret Friend pep talks every day, but just as Eric had predicted, nothing had changed.

All he had noticed so far was a lot of people sneaking pieces of candy onto empty desk tops, which seemed pretty silly. Except for Francine Topp. He knew by now that she was Bonnie Wong's Secret Friend, because she was always dropping little handmade presents on Bonnie's desk. And she had volunteered to take Bonnie's homework to her when she'd been sick.

Eric had racked his brain trying to think of what kind of Secret Friend thing he could do for Cynthia, but that was hopeless. Why had it been his fate to pick her name?

Since she'd been acting so unfriendly, he had to hurry to the lunchroom every day so he'd be lost in the crowd and wouldn't have to sit by her again.

It was getting complicated. He had to avoid Tyler and also, now, Jeremiah. No use risking more humiliation.

When the bell rang for lunch, he had just been plotting his lunchroom strategy when he saw Miss Arthur's blue eyes focused on him.

"Eric," she said softly, putting out her hand as he started for the door. "Eric, may I see you for a minute?"

Oh, sure. Great timing, Miss Arthur.

"I'm really pleased with your work, Eric," she said, leafing through her black grade book. "You're at the top of the class in math. And your written assignments in your other subjects show me that you know the material. With a little more classroom participation, you can get almost straight As this quarter. Do you think you could try a little harder?"

Eric shrugged his shoulders and glanced at the backs of the last classmates disappearing out the door. "I guess so," he said. He hoped it wasn't exactly a lie. He didn't like to lie to someone as nice as Miss Arthur.

"I was hoping you'd be feeling comfortable by now," she said, and her voice really sounded concerned. "We do try to care about each person here at Light of Life. I want all my students to feel that, Eric. And I know it can be hard when you're new. Have you made some friends?"

"Oh, sure." Eric felt as if he were dangling on the end of a fishhook and made a desperate effort to free himself. "I like it fine here, Miss Arthur." He even forced himself to look her straight in the eyes. "And I really do intend to participate more. I will. Honest."

He edged away—not enough to be rude, but just enough to let her know he was in a hurry.

"All right, Eric. That will be great. I'm sorry I kept you from lunch. You can go now."

Eric hurried to get his coat and lunch from the coatroom, but by now everyone else was gone. It was no surprise when he found that the only spaces left in the lunchroom were the ones around Cynthia Jebber. He slipped into the chair across from her and unwrapped his sandwich.

Cynthia had an open paperback in front of her and

was turning pages with one hand while she spooned tiny bites of yogurt into her mouth with the other. She might as well have put up a DO NOT DISTURB sign.

Eric picked up his sandwich carefully so the chunks of meat loaf wouldn't fall out. At least he wouldn't be choking on peanut butter this time. He bit into the sandwich and wished he had put on more mustard. He set it down on the plastic wrap and tried a bite of apple, getting more and more uncomfortable.

Even while Cynthia was reading, he felt as if she were staring. But no, her head was bent forward. A little bunch of dark curls had fallen over her forehead, and her eyelashes swept at a low angle. But he noticed that she hadn't turned a page for a long time.

"Good book?" Eric's voice surprised him. He had definitely not planned to say anything.

Cynthia lifted her head slightly, and he saw her dark eyes glaring at him.

"Who wants to know?" she snapped.

Oh boy. He should have kept his mouth shut, but it was too late now. "I was just asking," he said. "Sorry I bothered you." He picked up his sandwich, as though he didn't care in the least, and started to take a bite. Of course, that was just when a huge chunk of meat loaf, as though it had a life of its own, leaped away from the bread and bounced off the table and onto the floor.

His cheeks started burning, and as he leaned—undecided as to whether to pick up the meat or pretend it hadn't happened—he could hear a muffled snicker from Cynthia's side of the table. He straightened up, but by that time her face was grim again. He reached for his apple.

"You mean you're not going to pick that up?" Cynthia's voice was loud—loud enough to make the people at the other tables look. "You mean you're just going to let that big piece of meat lie there on the floor for someone to step on? How gross! Where were you brought up?"

Everyone had turned to look, and now even his ears were on fire.

"Hey, what's going on over there—a food fight?" yelled Tyler Wayne. "Whoever threw it is gonna be in big trouble."

"Better pick it up," Cynthia's voice prodded, sharp and smarmy.

Eric shoved back his chair and made a quick grab for the meat loaf. He would have liked to stay down and hide under the table, but he didn't have much choice. Still red-faced, he hid the meat in his lunch bag and tried to wipe his greasy fingers. He had forgotten to pack a napkin.

The laughter died down and some of the kids were leaving for the playground. Jeremiah was walking out with Tyler Wayne. Eric looked at his half-eaten apple.

He didn't feel like finishing it now. Across from him, Cynthia had finished eating but had closed her book and watched him, an amused expression on her face.

"What's the matter, Eric Bonner?"

So she knew his name. She took the trouble to know his name, and then embarrassed him like that. He wouldn't answer her. She didn't deserve an answer.

"Funny how that meat jumped right out of the bread. I've never seen anything like it," Cynthia said smugly. "Almost like . . . *voodoo*."

Like she was taking credit for his misfortune! To think that all the time he'd been feeling sorry for her!

"Creep!" he said between his teeth.

The half-smile left her face and she glared again.

"Fine," she said. "I'm a creep. Just consider us even."

"Even? I'm sure! What did *I* ever do to *you?*"

"You know what you did!"

"I never did anything. I talked to you once last week, that's all."

"What was that? Your good deed for the day?"

"You did most of the talking. I was just trying to be . . . friendly."

"You were friendly, all right. I may have some trouble walking, but I don't have any trouble seeing. You sure cut out in a hurry when you thought your friends noticed you sitting by me."

"My friends?" What was she talking about? As if he *had* some! Eric shook his head, not understanding. Cynthia just sat there, waiting, while he tried to recall that day a week ago. He had been so upset with Jeremiah's snub that he hadn't given much thought to Cynthia. Then he remembered Jeremiah in the lunchroom: the look he had given Eric as he walked past, the way Eric had cut short his conversation with Cynthia.

"Oh," he said. "That was nothing personal. You didn't have to get mad about that."

Cynthia's face was calm now. Calm and distant. She pushed back her chair and reached down to adjust her braces.

"I misjudged you," she said slowly as she pulled herself to her feet. "Somehow I had the idea you might care about people's feelings. But you don't, and from now on, neither do I."

Chapter 6

It was a relief to find that Mr. Robinson had saved him
a seat on the bus that afternoon. Eric collapsed into it
and buried his chin inside his puffy coat.

"Looks like you had a bad day, Eric," Mr. Robinson
said.

"I give up." Eric tried to burrow deeper.

"Ah, don't say that." Mr. Robinson patted his arm.
"They used to tell me and my wife to take it one day at
a time. Seems like you can always handle just one day.
Do you want to tell me about it?"

Eric shook his head. "It's too complicated. I try
making friends, but I only make things worse, whatever
I do."

"Like . . . ?"

"Did you ever make someone feel bad without knowing you did it?"

"Oh, I suppose that could happen easily enough." Mr. Robinson smoothed the corner of his mustache. "You just have to try to make up for it later."

"How can I? She's so mad she won't talk to me any more. And remember my teacher's great Secret Friend idea I told you about? Guess what? I'm supposed to be this girl's Secret Friend."

"Oh my. That *is* a problem. What had you planned to do for her?"

"I hadn't decided. A lot of kids are putting candy on desks. I don't think that's . . ." Eric stopped, not knowing exactly how to say what he meant.

Mr. Robinson just sat there and waited. Didn't butt in or try to finish the sentence or anything. Just waited.

"See, Miss Arthur wrote this thing at the top of the blackboard. It says, 'We may not see the good in others until we offer them our own goodness.' I don't really understand that."

"I'd say that takes some thinking about," Mr. Robinson agreed.

"It doesn't sound like she means giving candy or presents, does it?"

Mr. Robinson looked thoughtful. "It seems to me," he said slowly, "that I read something along those lines in the Bible once. Something about making peace with your neighbors before you bring your gifts."

"Then I'm really in trouble. I told Cynthia I hadn't meant it personally—what I did—but that didn't help. She's still mad."

"I guess it must have been personal to *her*. It will probably take a good bit of peacemaking. I'll bet your mother can give you some suggestions."

Eric tensed up. He studied the smooth gray vinyl of the seat in front of him. Tough, neutral vinyl. Untorn.

"I can't tell my mother," he said.

"Can't tell her?" Mr. Robinson looked amazed. "Why, that's what mothers are for—to help you understand things better."

"If I tell her, she'll think I'm not getting along in the new school. Then she'll get upset again."

"You don't have to say you're not getting along. Just ask for a little advice. Everybody wants advice."

"That's why I asked you," said Eric, almost whispering.

Mr. Robinson shook his head. "I'll tell you, Eric, my advice wouldn't be worth a plug nickel to you. Some things you have to learn in your own times, not from some old gramps who got his answers out of the past."

Eric fixed his eyes on the nylon backpack lying on his lap, bulging with books. He picked up the strap, loosened and retightened the buckle.

I wish he would give me some answers, he thought. Past or not, I would do whatever he said.

But the only advice Mr. Robinson gave was to talk to his mother. That night Eric decided to give it a try.

"You know that Secret Friend project we've got going at school?"

His mother looked up from the hem she was stitching. "Yes, you said something about it. It sounds nice. How's it going?"

"Well, this girl I got—Cynthia. Did I mention that she's disabled? Well, I've got this problem of not knowing what to do for her."

"Disabled? In what way?" his mother asked. She seemed more relaxed than usual.

"I forgot what it's called, but the kids say she's partly paralyzed. Even with leg braces and a cane, she can hardly walk."

His mother's mouth made a little, silent *o*. "That must be hard for her, with the stairs and all."

"Yeah, well, her mother brings her to school and takes her home. Some kids say she smells bad because she wears diapers, but I don't think that's true. It's just that she can't play outside at recess with us and stuff. She gets all *A*s."

"I was going to suggest that you help her with schoolwork." His mother smiled, even more relaxed now. "But I guess that's out."

"Besides, I guess I hurt her feelings. I didn't mean to, but now she's mad at me. Won't talk to me."

"Eric! That's not like you! I hope you didn't say anything about—"

"No, Mom! Definitely not. What happened was, I was talking to her, and when I saw some of the guys going out to recess, I got up and went, too."

Mrs. Bonner's eyes narrowed slightly. "Are you sure that's the whole story? I want you to think about it very, very carefully and decide if perhaps there's something you need to apologize for. You know, once you lose someone's trust, it takes a long time to gain it back."

"But Christmas vacation starts in a week, and I'm supposed to—"

"In the meantime," his mother said, interrupting, "why don't you buy a candy bar and leave it on her desk? That is, if you think she likes candy."

"Thanks, Mom. That's a good idea."

"And, Eric?" His mother leaned forward, her eyes all sparkly. "I'm glad you talked to me about this. It's a good sign. We need to be open with each other. This school is really working out better, isn't it?" Just a touch of wistfulness in her voice.

"Oh, sure. A lot." No matter what happened, Eric didn't want to see his mother upset again, like the day she dragged him out of the last school. "Everybody says Light of Life is the greatest, Mom."

*   *   *

Later, Eric sat on the edge of his bed, under his Quatre Cinq poster, thinking things out. Right now, he felt much better—talking to his mom had been a plus. Not that her advice had been so great. "Give Cynthia a candy bar." What an original idea! But then, Dad had been the one with neat ideas; Mom was the practical, dollars-and-cents person.

One thing he had learned tonight: By starting the conversation, he was the one in control. And it had made his mom happy, too. He hated the way she talked to him sometimes, as though she were his big sister—his pal. She used that act to pry, and he always clammed up when she did it. His new strategy was a trick worth remembering. A definite plus.

The lies were minuses. He had always been truthful and despised liars. But when you talk to adults, how can you please them without lying? Telling Miss Arthur he would participate in class, telling his mother about his great school—both were falsehoods. Still, there had seemed no way to avoid them.

The scene Cynthia had created in the lunchroom had, at the time, seemed like a Class-A minus. He couldn't have imagined anything worse than the embarrassment he felt picking the meat loaf off the floor with her yelling at him and kids laughing. At recess, lots of kids came up to him and asked about it or made jokes;

but it turned out that almost none of them knew what had happened or had seen the meat loaf at all. Maybe it wasn't such a minus, after all.

And he guessed it was a good thing that Cynthia had told him what she was angry about, even if he didn't agree that she had a reason. She was making a big deal out of such a little incident. There was no comparison with the way Jeremiah had left him, Eric, standing alone under the basket when Tyler called. It hadn't been the same at all. He and Cynthia had only been *talking*. With Jeremiah, they were starting a friendship when Jeremiah so rudely decided to call it off.

"I guess it must have seemed personal to her," Mr. Robinson had said. Eric shook his head. He decided he'd been right in the first place. There were all kinds of reasons he could never be friends with Cynthia. And they were even more complicated than he had thought at first. He just plainly could not understand her. He'd get up early and pick up a candy bar for her at the store tomorrow morning.

He had started getting ready for bed when another idea came to him. Cynthia liked poetry—Miss Arthur had praised something she wrote. Well, he could write poems, too. In fact, he had a half-filled notebook of his verses that no one had ever seen.

He reached under his bed for the shabby shoe box full of his personal things. When he untied the string and lifted the cover, the first thing he saw was the wedding picture. He bit his lower lip hard to keep from trembling as his father's bold eyes looked out at him. It was the only picture he had. He had rescued it from the trash right after his dad left and had torn it out of the folder so that it would fit in his box. His mother was in it, too, of course, but it didn't look like her. The bride in the picture was a starry-eyed blond teenager.

He sorted through the old birthday cards and other mementos until he found the notebook. Quickly, he glanced through the poems. Poems about being lonely. Odd poems about details and textures he had noticed around him. Cynthia would probably think he was weird. He would have to write a new one. He carefully retied the box and put it back under the bed.

Little bits and pieces were already floating around in his brain. It was just a matter of getting them in the right order and fitting five syllables in each line, of course.

He jotted them down in his school notebook, crossing out, rearranging. Squinting, he considered what he had written.

> *Candy's not healthy,*
> *but why not pretend*
> *it's from Quatre Cinq,*
> *your cool Secret Friend?*

Not perfect, but not bad, either. Lucky that he hadn't asked her if she liked Quatre Cinq. Then the verse would have given him away. But she was sure to know about Quatre Cinq. His albums were top sellers, and his concerts were always sellouts. And all because of magic.

Chapter 7

The next morning, things went exactly as Eric had planned. He took the early bus and got off at the grocery store, bought a Milky Way, and jogged the last three blocks to school. Although it was cold and there were snowflakes in the air, Eric was almost sweating when he got there. He hung up his jacket and glanced over to make sure Cynthia had not yet arrived. So far, so good. He held the candy and the folded page of poetry in his left palm, so he could brush lightly over the top of Cynthia's desk as he passed, leaving them without being noticed.

He sighed with relief as he slid in behind his initial-scarred golden oak desk. He had done it, and nobody had seen him. One by one, or two or three at a time, the kids were coming in the door. Jeremiah Peel ducked into the coat alcove to hang up his jacket, and just behind him was Cynthia's mother. And then Cynthia appeared, cane in hand, making her way slowly but persistently into the room. You had to give her credit. Simple movements were a major effort for her, but she didn't let anyone help her very often. She stopped and waited until her mother had hung up her heavy, blue cloak and then continued on toward her desk.

Once Cynthia sat down, Eric realized, he would be able to see only her back, and it suddenly seemed very important for him to witness her expression when she discovered his gift.

He grabbed two pencils out of his case and sped down the aisle in the direction of the pencil sharpener, keeping an eye on Cynthia all the way.

"Whoa, man, look out!"

Eric nearly collided with Jeremiah Peel, who had put out his hands to prevent a crash.

"Sorry. . . . 'Scuse me." Eric was sure his face must be turning red, but then he saw that Jeremiah was smiling. Not any secret half-smile, either, but a regular smile.

"Two-faced!" he wanted to yell but held it back.

"I wasn't lookin' " was what he said, surprising himself with his steady voice. "Sorry."

"That's okay. Take it easy, Bonner."

Eric continued down the aisle, almost forgetting

about Cynthia. By the time he reached the pencil sharpener and could see her face, she had already unfolded the paper and was reading it. She stared at it for a long time; and then, as Eric kept turning the handle for an already-sharpened pencil, a smile wreathed her face and stayed for a few seconds before fading. She refolded the paper and tucked it into the pocket of her folder.

"What're you doing, sharpening your arms?" taunted Tyler Wayne. Eric had not noticed him come in and ignored him, turning back toward his row. There was never any way to answer Tyler's barbs.

"Stick Boy, if you sharpen those arms and legs, you're gonna be a dangerous weapon. We'll have to watch out for you!"

"You just might have to," mumbled Eric, heading for his desk.

"Oh, listen to that . . . ," began Tyler, but noticing that Miss Arthur had come into the room, he closed his mouth and started to sit down. As he leaned over his desk, he grabbed up a package of Gummy Worms candy that had been lying there.

"Where'd this come from?" he growled. "I don't eat that cheap stuff." He flung the package of candy to the floor.

"Let's settle down back there." Miss Arthur's voice lost its honeydew quality for a second, and everyone quickly sat down.

It was a relief to recite the Pledge of Allegiance. If only they could spend the entire day learning from Miss Arthur, thought Eric, with no recesses, no lunch—only her bright voice holding them in its spell.

On Mondays and Thursdays they had geography and studied the major countries of the world. Each time, two students prepared a report. Today's country was China, and the report was so bad that Eric wanted to stuff his ears. The brightest kids had all volunteered first, so the reports were getting worse and worse. These two must have copied it all out of an encyclopedia. An *old* one at that.

Miss Arthur beamed at the two when they finished stumbling through their presentation.

"Thank you, Ann and Richard. That was very nice. You did a good job. Now, can anyone add more information about China?"

Bonnie Wong had already given a report on Great Britain but added some things her parents had told her about their Chinese ancestors. Then Miss Arthur skillfully summed up the most important points about China.

"Monday's assignment will be on Japan," she said at the end of class. "Six people have not yet given reports. Would someone like to volunteer?"

If they didn't, Miss Arthur would assign them. Japan was an interesting country. Eric already knew a little about it. Besides, maybe he could partly cancel out the lie he had told Miss Arthur about participating. He swallowed hard and raised his hand.

"Eric . . . very good. And who else? Oh, thank you, Jeremiah. We'll look forward to a fine report from you two on Monday."

Jeremiah? Eric bent forward, his hand holding his forehead. He could feel fine strands of hair hanging down, damp with perspiration. It had taken a surge of courage to get that hand in the air, but never in his wildest dreams had he expected Jeremiah to offer to be his partner! How was he supposed to handle all this? He knew that writing the report would be easy, but the thought of standing up in front of the class blew his mind. It would be worse than facing Tyler on the playground.

He sneaked a glance at Jeremiah, who was looking for something in his notebook. Was it a coincidence that Jeremiah had volunteered to work with him? He remembered the smile earlier. Maybe this would be a second chance for them to get acquainted. No, he wasn't going to start imagining anything like that again. He needed all his inner strength. No use in wasting it on letdowns.

When it was recess time, Eric noticed Francine lingering at her desk, pretending to rearrange her books. He knew what she was up to. He'd seen her do it before. As soon as Bonnie Wong left the room, Francine circled around past Bonnie's desk and left something small, wrapped in tissue paper. Then she hurried to catch up with the others, her face glowing.

The volunteer parent braved the icy wind to teach them a new game at recess. It was a relay, and the teams were chosen by counting off. Everybody had a chance, and neither team won every time. What a great world it would be, Eric thought, if only the fair people were in charge. If there weren't always people pushing others around, trying to get a bigger piece of the action for themselves. For once, recess was over almost too soon.

As they crowded back up the stairs, two boys who had never spoken to Eric before were next to him.

"Hey, Bonner, what was going on in the lunchroom yesterday?" one of them asked. "That chick with the cane was really giving you a hard time."

"It was nothing, really," Eric answered, embarrassed again.

"She sounded mad," said the other boy. "What is she, a psycho?"

The first boy laughed. "A schiz-o-phrenic." He drew the word out and twisted his face like a comedian.

"No, she's not." Probably Cynthia would have scorned his defense if she had heard him, but Eric thought it was the least he could do. "It was . . . my table manners. I guess I grossed her out."

"Oh yeah?" The boys exchanged snickers.

"If she ever sits at *our* table, she'll find out what gross really is, huh, Larry?" one of them said; and they both burst into laughter again, bumping shoulders against Eric, almost as though he were one of them.

When they returned to the classroom, Bonnie Wong squealed with delight as she tore away the tissue paper and found a tiny, framed teddy bear worked in counted cross-stitch. Francine, of course, looked the other way. As far as she was concerned, the Secret Friend project was working just fine.

Almost unconsciously, Eric checked the top of his own desk and then hated himself for looking. He had to admit that nobody had shown any signs of being his Secret Friend so far, but it didn't matter. Of course it didn't matter. He wouldn't have wanted to have one of those copycat candy givers for a Secret Friend, anyway. His Secret Friend, if he ever had one, would be above anything like that. Somebody just like Quatre Cinq. But, of course, he wouldn't find anyone like that in this classroom.

His immediate problem was to find a chance to talk to Jeremiah about the geography assignment, but the day passed with neither of them making a move. Well, there was still Friday, and they had all weekend to work on the project. Tomorrow would be soon enough.

Chapter 8

The bus got stuck behind a fender bender on the way to school, but someone's radio was playing "Santa Claus Is Coming to Town" and Eric found himself humming along. He stopped himself before anyone could notice, but the good feeling stuck. Today he was all psyched up for whatever might happen.

His mom had nearly flipped out last night when he casually told her about giving Cynthia the poem and candy bar. And then to top it all off, he'd told her how he and Jeremiah had volunteered to report on Japan. He hadn't seen her so happy since—well, for a long time.

Today he was going to talk to Jeremiah. There were plans to be made. This was important school stuff, and he would do it. For sure.

But when he got to school, he started getting cold feet again. Because of the bus delay, most of the kids were already in their seats. He hated walking past that row of eyes—being stared at like an insect under a microscope.

As he reached his desk, he saw the package of Gummy Worms lying there. There was no mistaking it. It was the very same package that Tyler Wayne had flung to the floor the day before. Eric didn't want to think about who had put it there. He covered it quickly with his hand and slipped it inside his desk when no one was looking.

What a bummer. If his Secret Friend had done this, his worst fears had come true. He would rather go unnoticed than to be given this trashed package of Gummy Worms.

He tried to put it out of his mind. He was doing okay, too, until recess, when out of the blue, Francine Topp jumped all over him.

"What kind of snitch are you?" she barked, her eyes flashing. "You just had to tattle, didn't you?"

Her words hit him like ice water. He had no idea what she was accusing him of.

"I—I don't know what you mean," he stammered.

"Don't play dumb. You watched me put those things on Bonnie's desk. Don't deny it. And then you had to go and tell her."

"I didn't tell." Eric felt his lips quiver. As if he would do anything to hurt Francine! But he had no more words to defend himself.

"Well, *somebody* told, and you're the one who's always sitting there like a zombie. You've spoiled everything." Without waiting for an answer, Francine walked away from him.

Talk about spoiling everything! Eric felt as though the floor had opened up under him. Francine's outburst had left him shaking. All his plans with Jeremiah suddenly seemed impossible. He doubted that he could even approach him, to say nothing about standing up to give that report on Monday.

For the rest of recess he kept his hands in his pockets, his fingers forming a desperate four-five position, but it didn't seem to help. Lately, his faith in Quatre Cinq's magic was getting pretty shaky. Maybe it didn't work for white dudes.

The day dragged on. On Friday afternoons they had art, and after that the weekly religion class. About half the kids went to it, and Eric tagged along. His mother said it was up to him, so since he was going to a Christian school, he figured he should have some idea of what they believed in. It was interesting, too, even though it seemed pretty farfetched.

Miss Arthur always read some verses out of the Bible and then would stop to explain them. Today she was telling about a guy named Isaiah. He wrote all these predictions back in olden days, before America was discovered. Before even Europe was discovered. And all the stuff he said had ended up in the Bible.

Then Miss Arthur asked questions, but it was all new to Eric. He didn't know any of the answers. Somehow it was supposed to tie in with Christmas—the story of Jesus in the manger.

"Isaiah the prophet foretold all these things before they happened," Miss Arthur explained, "but some people weren't sure what he meant. Who were some of the people who believed that the baby Jesus was really the savior?"

Lots of hands went up. "Mary." "Joseph." "The shepherds." Answers came from all directions.

"And the wise men," added Peggy Di Angelo. "They followed a star all the way from the Orient to bring presents."

Oh, yeah. Eric had heard that story before, but this time he was impressed. He had never really thought before how far they had to ride those camels to get there. *If* it was true.

When the class was over, they filed back to their own room. Cynthia had gone ahead, as she usually did, since she moved slowly. Richard Johnson led the rest of them and bumped the corner of Cynthia Jebber's desk, just as she was sitting down. Two spiral notebooks and a folder crashed to the floor.

Eric flinched. By the time Cynthia could manage to

get them picked up, they'd probably be a real mess. Everyone was leapfrogging over them, and some feet stepped right on them. No one stopped to pick them up.

Eric knew how he'd feel if they were stepping on *his* books. When he got there, he bent down and reached for the notebooks. The person behind him nearly slammed into him, but the rest made a wide circle to avoid him.

He plopped the notebooks on her desk. He wanted to say something friendly but was too embarrassed. Her eyes met his, but she quickly looked away.

"Thanks," she said coldly.

Well, what did he expect—gratitude? Eric knew he had better pull himself together. In less than two minutes they would all be going out the door. Miss Arthur was already starting her little end-of-the-week reminders.

Frantically, Eric tore off a corner of paper. "Call me tonight about the project," he wrote, and scrawled his phone number. It was the only chance he would have.

"Are all my Secret Friends getting ready for Christmas?" Miss Arthur was asking. "We're almost into the countdown. Have a good weekend!"

For once Eric didn't wait to be the last one to the coatroom. He hurried to catch up with Jeremiah and tapped his shoulder.

Jeremiah spun around, his brown eyes startled. When he saw it was Eric, he looked relieved.

"Here," Eric said, thrusting his note toward Jeremiah.

Jeremiah opened his left hand to take it. "Here," he said, and with his right hand shoved another piece of paper toward Eric. They both stepped back, out of traffic, to read the messages.

"Call me tonight. Phone 555-7982," said Jeremiah's note. They both gave a nervous chuckle.

"See ya," Jeremiah said.

"See ya," Eric said. He took his time putting on his jacket and headed for the bus stop.

The cheerful welcome from his elderly friends on the bus was like a warm blanket. He clung to its security until he reached the safety of Mr. Robinson's seat.

"Hi ya, Champ. How's it going today?"

Eric shrugged and plopped into the seat. "Okay, I guess. Good and bad."

"I guess that's life." Mr. Robinson had a wise saying for everything. "Have to take the bitter with the sweet."

"Only three days of school left until vacation," Eric said.

"Then I suppose I won't be seeing you for a couple of weeks."

"Maybe I'll ride the bus if I don't have anything else to do. I signed up for the Y basketball league, but I'm not sure if I'll go."

Mr. Robinson looked surprised. "Oh, yes, you'll have

to go—a tall boy like you! And the skating rinks will be open. You'll have more things to do than ride the bus."

"I guess you're right." How was he supposed to tell Mr. Robinson you have to have a friend to do things with?

"Speaking of things to do . . ."

Eric slumped in his seat, hardly listening to Mr. Robinson rambling on the way he always did. It must be nice to be old and not have any problems. He never heard anybody in that AMOS group putting each other down.

He jolted to attention when he realized Mr. Robinson was asking him a direct question.

"Sorry, what?"

"I just said, if you want to go to the Christmas pageant with me on Sunday, give me a call."

"Uh . . . well, it's a kind of busy weekend. I have to meet Jeremiah to work on a school project."

"That's all right. Just thought I'd ask." Mr. Robinson was smiling, but there was a look of disappointment in his eyes, as though it had really mattered to him.

"You said Sunday?" Eric pulled out the paper with Jeremiah's phone number written on it. "We might be finished by then. I'll ask my mom. Why don't you write your number on this paper?"

Mr. Robinson took out his pen and carefully printed his name and phone number on the back of the paper. A few minutes later he pushed the buzzer for the next stop, and Eric slid out of the seat to let him into the aisle.

Before he moved toward the door, Mr. Robinson's fingers pressed right through the puffy jacket and squeezed Eric's shoulder. "I'll bet your mother is surely proud to have you for a son. I know I would be. Now don't forget. Call me about the pageant."

Eric watched out the window as the bus pulled away and Mr. Robinson headed toward his big elegant house. He walked carefully, as though one leg were hurting.

A friendly black couple named Marie and Arnold were in the seat behind Eric. Marie leaned forward.

"Grant Robinson's a real nice man, isn't he?" she said. Her eyes shone warmly through her glasses. "I can tell he thinks a lot of you. He misses his wife, and his own grandchildren are so far away."

"Does he live in that big house all by himself?" Eric asked.

"Oh my, no," Marie said. "That's a rooming house—must be fifteen people living there. He just has one room. We try to get him out as often as possible."

"Yes, he is nice," Eric said. "I might go to the pageant with him."

After he got home and started cleaning up the kitchen, Eric, as he usually did, relived the day. He had started out feeling so confident. What had caused things to go wrong, again?

The memory of the Gummy Worms on his desk still made him feel sick. And Francine's false accusation—that was something he wanted to blot out forever. Why didn't she understand that he was not the kind of person who would do something like that? Why didn't people ever bother to notice what kind of person he really was? It just wasn't fair.

He shoved the cereal box onto the shelf and slammed the cupboard door. Might as well think about the positive things. He had liked Miss Arthur's Bible stories, and in spite of his embarrassment, he was glad he had picked Cynthia's books off the floor. If she didn't appreciate it, that was her problem.

Best of all, when had he ever had the phone numbers of two people who were waiting for him to call?

He decided to call Jeremiah as soon as he finished his chores. He could just pick up the phone and dial, and then it would be done. No use sitting around getting nervous about it.

He was putting away the broom when the phone rang. Maybe his mother was calling to say she'd be late.

"Hello?"

"Hello, is Eric there?" It was a woman's loud voice, definitely not his mother's.

"Yes, this is . . . me."

"I'm calling for Jerry Peel. You've got some report you're supposed to do this weekend?"

"Yes."

"Well, I expect the best place to do it is at the Main Library. Can you be there tomorrow morning?"

"Yes."

"How about nine-thirty? Can you make it by then?"

"Yes."

"Now, make sure you're there, okay, young man? If I take the trouble to get Jerry over there, I don't want to be dealing with Mr. No-Show."

Eric sighed. "I'll *be* there," he said.

"Nine-thirty, then." The woman hung up.

She hadn't even identified herself. Was it Jeremiah's mother? If it was, Eric felt sorry for him. No wonder he looked scared sometimes.

So they'd be meeting at the library. Now he didn't have to worry about making the phone call. But he was disappointed, too. It would have been nicer talking to Jeremiah.

Eric's mother was a half hour later than usual.

"I just stopped at the Dairy Queen with a couple of other girls from the office. Had to unwind after this week!" she explained. "I just finished a very big project. I don't suppose old Waldo will give me any credit for it, but I broke my back over it and got it done ahead of schedule."

"So you can enjoy your weekend," Eric suggested.

His mother laughed. "And have fun cleaning, shopping, doing laundry!" But this time she didn't sound so bitter about it.

"Remember the report on Japan I told you about?" Eric asked later, as they ate dinner together. "I have to meet Jeremiah at the library at nine-thirty tomorrow to work on it."

"At nine-thirty? I've got some things to do—," Mrs. Bonner began.

Eric interrupted her. "It's all right. I can take the bus. I know which one to take."

"Of course you do!" His mother's blue eyes glowed. "Sometimes I forget how capable you are. I'm really proud of you, Eric."

Proud! He could hardly believe his ears. That was exactly what Mr. Robinson had said.

She was not quite so enthusiastic when she heard about his invitation to join Mr. Robinson at the Christmas pageant. The old suspicious look came back as she gave him the third degree.

"What do you really know about someone you meet on the bus? Just because he has friends is no reason to automatically trust him. Besides, what do you know about the friends?"

And Eric had no solid answers. He *knew* that Mr. Robinson was a good man. But he couldn't prove it.

"I'll have to sleep on that one," his mother said firmly. "It's my job to make sure you're safe."

Eric had to admit that she was right.

Chapter 9

His mother liked to sleep later on Saturdays, so Eric tiptoed around, fixing his breakfast and getting ready. He double-checked his bus schedule. He would make it to the library well before 9:30.

Just as he as pulling on his puffy jacket, he heard her stirring. He knocked lightly on her bedroom door.

"I'm leaving now, Mom," he said, and hurried out before she had a chance to answer.

It was cloudy again, with ice-tipped gusts that slashed his face like knives. Eric pulled his cap over his forehead and stared at the curb by the bus stop. It was smooth and yellow, and although there was no sun, the paint glowed in a way he hadn't noticed before. Like a symbol of hope, a golden promise. A tremor traveled up Eric's spine. Today this curb was an exciting place to be.

The bus arrived. It rolled to a clumsy stop, and Eric whipped through the dividing doors almost as fast as they opened. There were only a few passengers aboard, and the trip uptown took less time than he had expected. He hopped off.

This was great. Now he would have time to study some of the fine old uptown buildings. He tilted his head to admire a cornice, the stone elaborately carved in swirling ribbons that extended to a scowling lion's head at the corner of the roof.

At his own level, his glove skimmed the marble smoothness of a cornerstone dated nearly a hundred years before. A hundred years! It was funny to think how a person's life could crumble in a single year, while something like a building could sit here, staying just the same almost forever.

But he was soon distracted. The shop windows were ablaze with Christmas decorations. Merchandise on display made his eyes pop. Even so early in the day, a good number of shoppers were already headed for the Center Point Mall, a block from the library.

He paused at a boutique, looking at the jewelry. A large pair of yellow enamel ear hoops made him think suddenly of Cynthia, which was strange. Cynthia never wore anything like that. They would look good on her, though.

Eric had not bought his mother a Christmas present yet, either. She had told him to wait.

"We'll go next Friday afternoon—just before Christmas Eve," she said. "We can get things for practically half price then."

He was sure she was right and that the gifts would be every bit as good. But wouldn't it be really special to walk into one of those stores today, choose something from the plentiful stock, and pay the full price, whatever it was, just because you wanted it for someone you loved?

He was attracted to a display of fine woolen scarves and mittens, and immediately thought of Grandma and Grandpa Bonner. With a painful frown, he turned away. His grandparents were still back in Minnesota, and somehow his mother had divorced them as well as his dad.

He glanced at his watch and saw that it was 9:20.

Pushing his knit cap up a little so his ears showed, he sauntered toward the library. His eyes measured the distance up the steps, and he forced himself not to hurry. He was starting to feel nervous, so he recited some Quatre Cinq lyrics over and over again. It helped a little. The wind whipped his face as he climbed the steps, but he plodded on as though he didn't notice.

When he pushed open the heavy glass door, the contrast of warm air nearly pushed him backward. He stood still to get his bearings and looked around, just in case Jeremiah was already waiting.

Then he went on, past the checkout counters and in

the direction of the reference area. He found a table and dropped his backpack on it. He sat down and took his notebook out of the pack and pretended to study it. Now it was up to Jeremiah Peel to find him. He sneaked a look at his watch. It was exactly 9:30.

"Hey, Bonner."

Eric looked up at the hoarse whisper and saw Jeremiah weaving toward the end of the table.

"Am I late?" Jeremiah lurched into a chair and slid awkwardly out of his jacket.

"Nah," whispered Eric. "How's it goin', Peel?"

Jeremiah's nose was oozing. He pulled out a gray hanky and blew several times until he had cleared it. Then he squirmed in his chair and stared at Eric.

"So what do we do now?" he asked.

"I suppose we'll have to look up Japan in the card catalog, or maybe the librarian can help us do a computer search."

"Oh . . . yeah. Or how about an encyclopedia?"

"Uh . . . sure. We can look there, too." Eric could tell when kids copied out of the encyclopedia, and he wasn't going to do that. But he didn't want Jeremiah to think he was some kind of nerd.

He stared at his notebook for a minute.

"Maybe we could divvy it up," he suggested. "Like I could write about the geography, and you could write about the history. Then I could do the customs, and you

could find out about their present system of govern-
ment."

"Oh, jeez." Jeremiah's bottom lip drooped and panic
showed in his brown eyes. "I'd rather just work on
everything together."

"Well, er, that's all right with me. Only it will take
longer that way."

"You got other stuff to do today?" Jeremiah asked.
Eric shook his head.

"Me either." Jeremiah grinned. "I can stay all day if
I want to. I just have to call home when I want to leave."

A man at the next table frowned at their whispering,
and Jeremiah stood up suddenly.

"C'mon. Let's find the bathroom," he whispered,
and Eric followed him.

Seeing him from the back, Eric noticed Jeremiah in
different ways than he had before. Maybe it was just
because it was Saturday, away from school, but Jeremiah
looked a little grubby. For instance, his blue-and-white-
striped T-shirt must have been washed with darker colors too often. His brown hair clung in strands and
needed cutting. Jeremiah was much shorter than Eric,
and stockier. Well, everyone was. But there was a sort
of jolting bravery in the way Jeremiah moved, even when
he was going in the wrong direction, as he was now.

"Wait up," Eric whispered. "I think it's the other
way."

Jeremiah stopped short, looking confused. Eric jerked his head toward the passageway where he had seen rest room signs, and they were off again.

When they were inside, Jeremiah leaned against the wall and cleared his throat.

"Libraries get to me," he said. "Don't they you?"

"I don't know," Eric said.

"I mean, not being able to talk out loud. And all those books! Who would ever read all of them?"

"Nobody reads *all* of them. But they have to be there, for when somebody comes looking for something. Like us. I thought you had to go to the bathroom."

Jeremiah glanced toward the urinals. "Not really," he said. "I just wanted to talk out loud. About our report."

"Oh. Well, maybe a librarian can help us find some stuff."

Jeremiah looked shocked. "Wouldn't that be cheating?"

" 'Course not! That's what they're s'posed to do." Eric was beginning to feel more confident. He could see that he would be leading Jeremiah through this project.

"Was that your mother who called last night?" he asked. It was hard to connect Jeremiah with that strident voice.

"Yeah. Well . . . no. She's my foster mother."

Eric was afraid to ask another personal question, but Jeremiah seemed moved to explain.

"It's temporary, see. My mother died and my father . . . well, he can't take care of us right now. So I live with this lady who takes foster kids. She's got a son of her own, and three foster kids."

"You got *real* brothers and sisters?"

"Just a sister. She lives with my grandmother, but there wasn't room for me. My grandmother's rich. She's the one who pays my tuition."

"Ever see your father?"

Jeremiah wet his lips nervously. "Not too often," he said. "See, he's the captain on a merchant ship, and he hardly ever gets back here."

"Wow!" Eric was impressed. "Maybe when you're older, you can go to work on his ship."

Jeremiah nodded. "That's what I'm going to do," he said firmly. "As soon as I'm out of high school, I've got a job waiting for me on his ship."

"Does he ever go to Japan?"

Jeremiah's nervousness disappeared. "Oh, sure. All the time. I'll bet he could tell us all about it. Only, like I say, he never gets back here much."

"I don't see my dad, either," Eric said. "They got divorced last year and my mom has full custody. There's just the two of us. We moved here before school started."

"Bummer," Jeremiah commented, and Eric nodded agreement. They looked at each other with mutual understanding, and Jeremiah blew his nose again.

"Well," said Eric, "as long as we're in here, I might as well go."

He walked over to the urinal and unzipped his jeans.

A second later, Jeremiah was standing beside him, and as the two streams of pee gurgled down the drain together, both of them snickered.

"Hon-or-able Jap-a-nese cus-tom," mimicked Eric, and they collapsed in bursts of laughter.

Chapter 10

A librarian helped them find a few good reference books and then showed them the periodical index on the computer. Eric stood back and let Jeremiah scroll through the listings on Japan.

"Far out!" Jeremiah jiggled with excitement as his finger controlled the computer. "Who would have thought I'd get to be a computer whiz? You want a turn, Eric?"

Eric shook his head. "That's all right. You're doing great, Jeremiah. That one looks like one we can use. Push the print button."

The printer chattered out the information while Jeremiah watched in amazement.

"We worked on computers once a week at my other

school," Eric explained. "I guess Light of Life can't afford them."

They printed out about ten possibilities, located them in the periodical files, and brought everything to their table. By noon Eric's outline was filled in with figures, messy notations, bits and pieces of information.

Jeremiah worked hard, too, struggling through pages of data, dutifully recording it with a pencil that seemed to wear down to wood every five minutes. They were a long way from a neat report.

They decided to take a lunch break. Jamming everything into Eric's backpack, they grabbed their jackets and headed out of the building. It hadn't warmed up any. In fact, the wind seemed even colder than before.

Jeremiah hunched his shoulders as he walked, and the cold air made him cough. Eric had never really noticed Jeremiah's winter jacket before. It was brown corduroy, and didn't look very warm. Eric hunched his shoulders too. It wouldn't hurt to let Jeremiah think his new quilted jacket let in the cold as well.

The mall was crowded with customers, but they were lucky to find a table at a fast food place, where they could eat their burgers and fries. Eric took tiny bites. He wanted this lunch to last a long time. His first Saturday lunch in the mall with a friend.

"Your foster home—what's it like?" he asked.

Jeremiah shrugged. His chin jutted out a little. "It's okay. I get along with them. They don't hit me or anything—the other guys, I mean. Annie—my foster mother—won't stand for fighting."

"Do you have a room of your own?"

"No way. But it's not too bad. Kevin and me have bunk beds in our room. He's only eight. I don't mind him, except when he gets into my stuff. I s'pose you've got your own bedroom."

Eric nodded. "It's small, though," he said.

They were quiet for a minute.

There were so many things Eric wanted to know. Things he *needed* to know. Like how Jeremiah found ways to "get along" when he, Eric, couldn't.

"Do you like it at Light of Life?" he asked.

Jeremiah shrugged, just as he had before. "It's okay."

"Miss Arthur's a neat teacher, don't you think?"

"Yeah, she's pretty cool."

"What about Tyler Wayne? Is he a friend of yours?"

Again Jeremiah's chin jutted forward. "Sure. I get along with Tyler Wayne."

"I don't." It was reckless, but Eric said it, anyway.

Jeremiah took a big bite of his hamburger. "You should," he said, with his mouth full.

"Oh, sure," Eric said. "He hates my guts."

Jeremiah finished chewing and shook his head. "No, he just thinks you ain't *got* any. He only picks on people that are afraid of him."

Eric frowned. He already knew that. But what could he do about it?

"He's not going to hit you," Jeremiah went on. "He's too scared of getting caught. If he ever gets into trouble at school, his folks whip the daylights out of him."

"How do you know that?"

"From one of the guys that knows his family."

Now that he thought about it, it made sense. Tyler was always putting on his 'good boy' act when Miss Arthur was around. Just knowing that might help.

They finished eating and slurped the last drop of cola out of the ice.

"I gotta call Annie," Jeremiah said. "I told her I'd call if we weren't finished by twelve-thirty."

"I should call, too," agreed Eric. He thought again about the mishmash of stuff on Japan in his backpack. "I sure wish . . ."

"What?"

"Well, I was thinking how hard it's going to be, deciding how to write this, having to whisper all the time. And then we need to practice presenting it for class on Monday. Do you think your foster mother would let you come over to my house? I'll bet my mom could drive you home later."

"She might. I could ask."

"I know what. I'll call first, and if my mom says it's all right, then you can call."

When Eric called, his mom acted as if he had been accepted into the astronaut program, and *of course* she would drive Jeremiah home.

Jeremiah's foster mother wanted to know where Eric lived.

"On the west side," Eric whispered. "Not far from John Adams High School."

"Oh, yeah?" Jeremiah sounded surprised and talked into the phone and to Eric at the same time. "John Adams High School. That's not far from Webb Village housing, where *we* live."

When he hung up, he grinned at Eric. "Annie has to take her son to work right now, so she'll pick us up here in a few minutes and drive us to your house."

The car that pulled up in front of the mall was an old boat with faded green paint and a sagging tail pipe. The heavyset woman driver had a scarf tied over her curlers and was smoking a cigarette.

"Eric, why don't you sit in the backseat with Kevin?" she suggested cheerfully as they opened the heavy car door. "We've only got two seat belts in front."

"Okay." Eric untangled one of the backseat belts and put it across his lap. A cloud of cigarette smoke floated back and made him cough. The little boy named Kevin giggled, and Eric smiled at him.

"So you live out near us on the west side, huh?" the woman asked, turning her head slightly in Eric's direction. She maneuvered the big car skillfully through the traffic. "You'll have to give me directions to your house."

"We live in an apartment on Webster. Right off the bus line," Eric said. "Twenty-two oh seven."

"Just past Jensen's Greenhouse? Sure, I know where it is." Jeremiah's foster mother took another drag on the cigarette.

Eric waited for the cloud of smoke and raised his backpack in time to ward off the worst of it. Kevin giggled again. Easy for him to laugh—he was on the upwind side.

"Well, you two guys had better do a good job on this report," the woman continued. "God knows Jerry needs the grade. Every time his grandmother calls, she wants to know how he's doing in school. Now she's getting copies of his report cards, and I can't say she was too pleased last time. Right, Jerry?"

Jeremiah just shrugged. He looked embarrassed.

"You seem to get a lot of homework at Light of Life," she went on. "Jim is in the eighth grade in the public school. He don't get near as much homework as Jerry."

Eric didn't know if he was supposed to answer, but he decided she was one of those people who can't stand silences. She just kept talking and didn't seem to care who listened.

When she stopped the big car in front of his building, she reached over and patted Jeremiah's hand.

"You come home before supper, now. Don't be imposing on Eric's mother, or she won't want to have you back. And mind your manners. Wipe your nose when it needs it."

Jeremiah nodded and opened the car door.

"Good-bye, Mrs. . . . er . . ." Eric realized he still hadn't been told her name.

"Just call me Annie. Everybody else does," she said. The door slammed and the car roared away.

"Well, this is it," Eric said. The narrow strip of grass in front was frozen and brown, and the building looked drabber than ever.

"Pretty nice!" Jeremiah sounded as though he meant it.

Eric's mother must have been cleaning, because he smelled Pine Sol even before he opened the apartment door. A good, clean smell.

"Hi, Mom. This is my friend Jeremiah." Had he really said that? Or was it all a daydream, like the ones he had on the bus sometimes?

"Come in, Jeremiah." Eric knew his mother well enough to recognize the quick appraisal as she greeted Jeremiah, but she acted friendly. She wore a pink smock over her jeans and had put her hair in a ponytail for doing housework. She looked sort of young and pretty—almost like the girl she'd been in the wedding picture.

The kitchen table was shining clean, ready for them to lay out their notes on Japan. The teakettle was steaming, and two cups and a canister of instant cocoa waited on the counter.

After Jeremiah had blown his nose again, trying to be discreet, they got to work. They discussed each sentence and took turns writing on fresh paper. Jeremiah was more helpful than Eric had expected, once he got into it.

When they reached the part on Japanese culture, Jeremiah grinned mischievously and whispered, "Honorable Japanese custom!"

They both doubled over laughing, and Eric's mother asked, "My goodness, what's so funny?" They just laughed twice as hard.

At last they finished the report, drank the cocoa, and practiced how they would give the report in class on Monday.

"Maybe if we take turns, a little bit at a time, it will be easier," Eric suggested.

Jeremiah was ready with his pencil to mark the places. "It might not be so boring that way," he agreed.

"I like the way you toss it back and forth," Eric's mother said, listening to them rehearse. "Just like a team of newscasters on TV."

They went over it three times, until it was smooth. Eric sneaked a look at the clock. There was still a little time left before Jeremiah would have to leave.

"Wanna see my room?" he asked.

"Sure."

Of course, the first thing Jeremiah noticed was the Quatre Cinq poster.

"Hey I know who that is. Isn't he the one that does 'That Sinking Feeling'?" Jeremiah asked.

"Yes, it's Quatre Cinq." Eric tried to say the name with a French accent, but it was hard to do. It came out like "Cat Sank." "I like all his stuff."

"Yeah, he's good. I like Nigel Samson. He does rap."

"He's good, too."

"My African-American foster brother says that's black music, so *he* can like it, but *I* shouldn't. Do you think that's true?"

"Of course not," Eric answered. "How can music be black or white? If it's good, I like it. Just like people."

"That's what I think, too. What do you think of that black girl in our class—that Cynthia?"

Eric stared at Jeremiah, surprised at the question. "How come you asked that?" he asked.

"No reason. I thought I saw you talking to her a couple of times. Seems like nobody likes her. That's not because she's black, is it?"

"I don't think so," Eric said. "The other black kids in class get along all right." He didn't want to tell Jeremiah the real reason the kids stayed away from Cynthia if he didn't already know.

"I guess they think she's kind of weird," he added.

"She's okay when you get to know her, though. And she's really smart." There. He'd done another favor for Cynthia, whether she knew it or not.

"I hope my mom gets me a boom box for Christmas," Eric went on, changing the subject. "I'd like to tape some of Quatre Cinq's songs."

"That'd be neat. Annie's son has one, but I never get to play it. He likes all heavy metal."

They went back to the kitchen and saw that it was time for Jeremiah to go home.

"By the way," Mrs. Bonner said as she reached for her warm coat, "I called your friend, Mr. Robinson, this morning."

Eric gasped. He had completely forgotten about going to the pageant with Mr. Robinson on Sunday.

"Don't worry," his mother assured him. "He sounded very nice on the phone, and I suggested we should all go to the pageant together tomorrow afternoon. I can drive and pick up Mr. Robinson, so you won't have to take the bus. Is that all right?"

"Oh, that would be great! Thanks, Mom."

"And how about you, Jeremiah? Would your mother let you come with us too? We'd love to have you."

Eric held his breath. But Jeremiah's narrow face was bobbing up and down in a Yes motion, and his wide, brown deer eyes were not wary at all.

Chapter 11

By Sunday afternoon Eric's mother had practically worn a path to the window, checking the weather.

"I don't like this at all," she kept saying. "This could turn into a real blizzard."

"No chance." Eric tried to sound convincing. "It's getting warmer—the snow will melt right off. Besides, it's not that far to drive." Didn't she understand how important it was to him to go to this concert after making plans with Jeremiah and Mr. Robinson?

"I can't afford to take chances," she said. "If I smashed up the car, I'd really be in a fix."

"You won't, Mom. You're a good driver."

But Eric knew the weather, not his words, would be the deciding factor. At times the big sticky snowflakes were so thick you could hardly see through them. Then again they would nearly stop, floating past the window like lazy white feathers.

At two o'clock it was hardly snowing at all, and Eric was at the door, wearing his jacket and urging his mother to hurry. What a relief to be finally on their way!

Mr. Robinson was waiting on the big front porch of his rooming house. He was wearing a furry black hat and a long, striped scarf wrapped around the collar of his overcoat.

"He's very well dressed," Mrs. Bonner remarked. "He has a certain European style about him."

Eric didn't say anything. When his mother said weird things like that, he usually ignored them. It was just plain old Mr. Robinson, after all.

He got out and held the front car door open. Mr. Robinson came down the sidewalk carefully, but he wasn't limping today. He wore little, low-cut rubbers over his shiny black shoes.

"Well, Mrs. Bonner, I am very pleased to meet you," Mr. Robinson said, tilting his white mustache toward Eric's mother as he climbed into the seat beside her. "It looks a bit like winter today, doesn't it?"

Eric scrambled into the backseat. As they drove off, his mother and Mr. Robinson carried on a lot of boring grown-up small talk, but he didn't mind too much. In only a few minutes, he would have Jeremiah to talk to.

It had been almost dark the night before when they took Jeremiah home, and Eric hadn't noticed what a slum he lived in. Now, in the daylight, the Webb Village housing development really looked run-down and shabby. Garbage cans were out on the curb, and loose rubbish was scattered around. The buildings themselves were not too bad, except that there were so many, so close together.

They pulled up in front and Mrs. Bonner tapped the horn. Eric stared at the entrance, waiting. In just a minute Jeremiah, wearing his corduroy jacket, hurried out. Just above his head, to one side, was a large sign: NO PETS ALLOWED IN THIS BUILDING.

Jeremiah jogged toward them, snowflakes catching in his stringy hair. He jumped into the backseat beside Eric, and they exchanged grins. Just like friends.

"Is your cold better today, Jeremiah?" Mrs. Bonner asked.

"Lots better," Jeremiah said, snuffling.

Eric remembered to introduce him to Mr. Robinson; but something was bothering him, and as soon as he had a chance, he blurted out his question.

"Where do you keep your dog?"

Jeremiah wrinkled up his nose. "My dog? I don't got a dog."

"The German shepherd. You know, the one you told Tyler Wayne about."

"Oh, *that* dog." Jeremiah had a sudden coughing spell, and when he had recovered, he pretended to look toward Eric without actually meeting his eyes. "Well, what I said was, I *used* to have a dog. When I lived with my family. We can't have dogs at Webb Village."

"Oh, yeah." For a second, Eric wondered if he had misunderstood Jeremiah that day in the school yard. The scene flashed through his mind, and he was sure he hadn't. Jeremiah had told an outright lie that day and had just now told another one to cover up!

Then he remembered his own dishonesty with Miss Arthur and with his own mother. Maybe Jeremiah, who got along with everyone, sometimes felt cornered, just as he had.

On the main streets the snow had turned to slush, and it splashed up on the car as Mrs. Bonner drove toward the uptown area.

"I'm not sure I know where that church is. Do I stay on this street?" She turned to Mr. Robinson for advice.

"All the way to Third. Then you can take a right and start looking for a place to park. St. James Episcopal is the one with the big steeple. It's the biggest church in town—perfect place for this pageant. But all the other churches take part, too, you know. It's very ecumenical."

Eric wondered if his mother knew what that meant. He sure didn't.

She took a right on Third, and they looked for a parking place. After they had found one and started walking the four blocks to the church, they saw other vacant parking spaces much nearer. The snow was coming down faster again.

"Maybe some people stayed home because of the weather," Mrs. Bonner said.

"Oh, it's not so bad." Mr. Robinson didn't seem to be letting the slush bother him. His low-cut rubbers stepped right along next to Mrs. Bonner's stylish boots. "You boys still coming back there?"

Eric's thick-soled joggers stood up to the slush, but he noticed that Jeremiah's sneakers were getting soaked. That was not going to help Jeremiah's cold.

"We're early," Mr. Robinson said. "That's why the street isn't crowded yet. But it's good to be early. We can pick the choice seats."

"Wow!" Eric couldn't hold back the exclamation when they walked up the steps of the church. He was looking up at the elaborate figures carved in stone, set between the stained-glass windows. Sounds of instruments tuning floated out, mixed with snatches of choral harmonies—last-minute practices.

Jeremiah's brown eyes were wide, too.

"Jeez," he said.

It wasn't just the fancy architecture. Eric had seen stuff like that lots of times on TV. It was something else: an eerie feeling that they were entering another dimension.

His mother's heels clicking on the marble floor drew

Eric's attention, making his breath stop for a second. The lights, hanging on long chains from the arched ceiling, reflected the last melting snowflakes in her blond hair. They sparkled like diamonds in a tiara, and with her fine features and uptilted chin, she suddenly seemed every bit a queen. A half step behind, in Old World elegance, came her footman, Mr. Robinson.

Eric half expected a fanfare from the musicians, who were shuffling into their places in front. But when the queen bent to sit down in one of the long pews, the diamonds were gone, and it was only Mom in her tan wool coat.

Eric and Jeremiah settled into the pew directly behind. Mrs. Bonner turned around. "Stay right next to the aisle," she whispered. "If someone else wants to sit down, make them crawl over you. We were here first."

There were noises from the rear of the church, and Eric turned to see what was going on. Looking upward, he saw that the balcony, which stretched across the entire back, was filled with people, most in robes or costumes. They were crowded in front of the tall, gleaming organ pipes that reached toward the ceiling. Again, the height of that ceiling gave Eric a dizzy feeling, and his imagination kept playing tricks on him.

The pews were filling up now, too. Crowds of people were streaming in the doors. A well-dressed couple tried to make the two boys move over in their pew, but Eric clenched his teeth and politely motioned them to climb over.

"Man, you got nerve," Jeremiah whispered admiringly.

"I won't have to do it again, anyway," Eric whispered back. The rest of their pew was filled now, from the other end. In a few minutes, the program would begin.

Eric felt a hand on his shoulder. He saw that it was one of the ushers.

"Boys," the man whispered, "I'm afraid you'll have to move. It's urgent. I need seats for the mayor and his wife. Come, I'll find you another place."

We were here first, Eric wanted to say, but this time he couldn't. The mayor was an important person.

"Thanks so much, boys." The mayor's careful smile was the same one he used on television. Helplessly, Eric and Jeremiah moved out as the usher proudly seated the mayor and his wife.

Eric's mother hadn't even noticed what had happened. She was looking toward the front and talking to Mr. Robinson.

The two boys exchanged glances. It was plain they'd been picked on just because they were kids. There were no other seats, of course. They had to stand with latecomers who lined the rear walls.

The orchestra up in front burst into a great, brassy introduction, and choirs from all sides of the church joined voices. And when the huge, deep-voiced organ pipes from the loft above him rumbled, it made Eric shiver. He wanted to press close to Jeremiah, but someone had pushed between them. Here, in the midst of this overflow crowd, he suddenly felt all alone.

He tried focusing on some of the people around him, but in the shadows cast by the balcony, they seemed like scary figures, with only their teeth and eyeballs catching glints of light. He closed his own mouth and lowered his eyelids.

Through the overpowering music, Eric heard a stir of footsteps overhead—then descending, descending. All those eyes turned toward a doorway, where the stairs came down from the balcony. In the doorway, Eric could see white folds and ripples of cloth. The music swelled to a grand ending; and at that moment, the white folds came forward—a band of winged angels, carrying harps and wind chimes.

With the last echo of brass and pipes, a thin cobweb of soprano voices began. The angels floated slowly past Eric. They were teenagers, not much older than he. One by one, new voices joined the first, in strange harmonies, still light and airy as the wind chimes. Yet Eric could still hear their song long after they had passed down the long aisle to the front. Were there really sounds like this in heaven? It was something to think about.

In staring after the angels, Eric had almost missed

the Holy Family. They paraded past him, following the angels down the aisle. New choirs had their turn to sing familiar carols as group after group filed down from the loft and up the aisle. There were shepherds, more angels (less musical than the first), and a choir of children dressed in smocks with big red bows tied under their chins.

Still more actors were coming down the stairs. How could so many have been up there, Eric wondered? Some boys in brown cloaks lifted a big cardboard camel and stood waiting. They peered anxiously up the narrow stairway.

The three Kings of Orient seemed to be having trouble. The heavy layers of their rich costumes brushed the walls. At last, two of them ducked through the door, but the third one's tall crown didn't quite make it.

Everyone gasped as it went clattering to the floor and spun across the shiny marble. Hands reached out for it and missed. Hardly thinking, Eric stuck out a damp shoe. The crown bounced against his heavy sole and stopped. He stooped and picked it up.

Someone tried to take it from him; but he held it, his slim fingers caressing the papier-mâché textures, the fake jewels. The King who had dropped it was in front of him now, and Eric was surprised to see that he was black. In his hands he carried a large golden bowl. His draped cloth headpiece was still in place.

The black King smiled at Eric. Not the kind of smile you would expect from a king. Definitely not a mayor smile. This big smile started in the shining dark eyes and wrapped right around Eric.

"Man, I am a real klutz," whispered the King. "S'pose you can lay that crown back on me? It fits between some little clips up there."

The King squatted down so Eric could fix the crown in place. When he stood up again, the other two Kings were already on the way down the aisle, but he took the time to grin again at Eric. Balancing the bowl in his left hand, he lifted his right hand, thumb folded in the palm. Then, with another distinct thrust, he spread all five fingers wide. The four-five sign!

"Peace to ya, man," he whispered. He did a quick dance step, turned, and hurried after the others.

Eric stood with his mouth open. He felt as though he'd been zapped with a thousand volts. The four-five sign. The dark face that had smiled so warmly. So familiar, so personal. He closed his eyes, and the images swirled and blended into the face on the poster in his room.

Of course! How come he hadn't recognized him right away? It was Quatre Cinq in disguise! For some reason, the singer had come to town to be in the pageant. And he, Eric Bonner, had put the crown on Quatre Cinq's head. He could feel his heart racing. He started to look for Jeremiah and heard his partly muffled cough close behind him.

Jeremiah poked him in the ribs. "Way to go, Bonner," he said.

Suddenly, the people around Eric seemed to come out of the shadows. Their eyes and teeth weren't scary at all. They were friendly, glad that he, Eric, had helped the King. And for the first time since the divorce, he felt proud and happy.

Chapter 12

Eric had dreamed all night about the black King. The feel of the jeweled crown still tingled on his fingers. But most of all, he felt the Power. He couldn't think of the right word for it, but there must be one. Something like magic had passed from that handsome King to himself. One thing was for sure: He would shut up about it being Quatre Cinq. He had said it just once.

"Well, of course it wasn't!" his mom had scoffed. "I'm sure Quatre Cinq wouldn't show up *here*!"

That had been on the way home. Between the slippery driving conditions and her anger that the mayor had taken the boys' seats, she had been grumbling all the way. He hoped Jeremiah, and especially Mr. Robinson, wouldn't think she was always so crabby. It was not a very nice ending for the pageant, which even *she* had to admit was beautiful.

It would be no use trying to explain that the loss of their seats was something *meant to be*—that it had led him to his *very special moment*. Mom just didn't understand things like that. In her life, everything came in small print.

Eric had planned to review his report on Japan during the bus ride to school, but when the time came, he decided it wasn't necessary. He and Jeremiah had gone over it again and again. Besides, they were friends now. When they got up there, they'd wrap it up—no sweat—just like they had on Saturday. They would just pretend the class wasn't watching.

Instead, he had an urge to write something. Something for Cynthia. He took out his notebook and rested his pen on the paper. His fingers followed the pen as though someone else was dictating the words. It was that easy.

> *I've learned that if we look around*
> *there is goodness to be found.*
> *Last night I heard the angels sing*
> *and did a favor for the King.*
> *He gave me a reward (it's true!)—*
> *and I will pass it on to you:*
> *The season's sign of peace I send*
> *from Quatre Cinq, our Secret Friend.*

At the bottom of the poem, Eric drew two hands, one with the thumb folded under. He tore the page out of his notebook and folded it. Of course, she wouldn't understand it, but somehow, it might mean something to her.

The bus had run a little late, and most of the kids were already at their desks. Too bad. He had wanted to double-check with Jeremiah. On his way back to his desk, Eric could feel Tyler Wayne watching him. When Eric was close enough to hear, Tyler turned in his seat, toward Jeremiah.

"Hey, Jerry, my buddy. Are you all ready to give your big report with Stick Boy?"

C'mon, Jeremiah—don't let him psych you out! Eric wished that Jeremiah would at least look at him. Together they could stand up to Tyler Wayne. But Jeremiah had a sudden fit of coughing, covering his face with his sleeve. Then he caught his breath, stumbled out of his seat, and rushed up the aisle to the front of the room.

What was going on, anyway? Jeremiah was leaning close to Miss Arthur's ear. She was frowning and nodding, and patting his shoulder. After a minute he returned to his desk, still not looking toward Eric, and Miss Arthur rang her little bell, signaling the start of class.

"In case any of you forgot, we have only two and a half days of school this week. Then you'll be off for winter break."

Everybody laughed. As if they could forget!

Miss Arthur went on. "Wednesday morning we're going to have a movie and gift exchange. Don't forget to bring the gift for your Secret Friend. Don't spend more than a dollar, remember. And put your name on the card, so your Secret Friend will know who's been doing all those nice things. If you haven't signed up yet to bring food for the lunch, be sure to do it. We'll start the Christmas lunch at eleven-thirty. At twelve-thirty, vacation starts!"

A muffled shout went up around the room, dying quickly as Miss Arthur indicated that she had something else to say. Her face looked very sweet and serious.

"Boys and girls, I want you to know how much I appreciate you. At first, when we started the Secret Friend project, I was . . . uncertain how it would go. But I've seen some wonderful things happening. I'm glad to see that my sixth-grade kids know that the best gift we can give is kindness and respect—any time of the year. Thank you for that."

She shook her light brown curls, as if to change her mood. Grabbing a songbook, she headed for the piano. "Now for some of your favorite Christmas carols!"

Eric opened his mouth and really tried to sing. Maybe singing would help bring back the way he had felt last night. But the sounds stuck in his throat. What was up with Jeremiah? The geography class was coming up next, and he felt that something was wrong. If only he knew what.

The songs were over. It was time for Japan. Eric's written report was neatly clipped together, and on top of it were the notes he had made for the oral presentation he and Jeremiah were to share. Still, Jeremiah would not give any sign that he was ready.

"Today Eric Bonner and Jeremiah Peel have prepared a report on Japan. Unfortunately, Jeremiah has laryngitis and won't be able to participate, but I'm sure Eric will do a fine job."

Laryngitis! So that was what the coughing was about. But why hadn't Jeremiah come over and told him? Eric remembered Tyler Wayne's teasing and the way Jeremiah had been sneaking around. Laryngitis, all right. He was just using his cold as an excuse. Jeremiah had chickened out, that was all.

Eric forced himself slowly to the front of the room. There was no way he could give this report by himself. He'd be stuck on Word One. He approached Miss Arthur.

"We planned this together," he whispered. "It just won't work alone."

"Maybe we can fix that," Miss Arthur said cheerfully, looking around the room. "May I have a volunteer to read Jeremiah's share of the report?"

There was a moment of silence. Then Tyler Wayne started waving his arm.

"Thank you, Tyler. Jeremiah, can you give Tyler your notes? This will work out just fine." Miss Arthur sat down, as if she were expecting Act I of *The Sound of Music*.

Eric cringed. Could anything be worse? He should have said he forgot it at home. Somehow, he had to get through it. He read the opening, but his voice was small and tight—nothing like when he and Jeremiah had practiced on Saturday.

"I can't hear," someone said in the back.

Eric tried to speak louder, but he just couldn't. The words were swimming before his eyes, and he didn't even know what he was saying. Somehow, he made it as far as the part that was supposed to be Jeremiah's.

Tyler's voice was very loud and he read every word separately, making it sound stupid. "We have . . . seen . . . pictures of . . . vulcanizers like . . . Mount Fudgey and . . ." At the sound of laughter, he stopped and looked around innocently.

"That's *volcanoes* like Mount *Fuji*," Miss Arthur corrected. "You can do better than that, Tyler."

"It's Jer's bad writing, Miss Arthur. He really needs to improve his penmanship," Tyler explained, and went on, skipping to another paragraph. "After the . . . twelfth cutlery . . . powder was held by the . . . shotguns." Laughter again, and Tyler made a comic face.

It was humiliating. All the work they had done on Saturday was being ridiculed. There was no point in even trying. Eric walked back toward his desk, fighting tears.

"That's enough, Tyler!" It was the first time Eric had seen Miss Arthur angry. "Sit down, Tyler, and let's hear the rest of Eric's report."

But Eric was back in his seat. She could call on him until she turned blue. He would not go up front again. He'd take an *F* first.

But Miss Arthur didn't call him again. Prepared as always, she went smoothly into her own interesting lecture on Japan. Eric closed his ears. He didn't want to hear it. He hated her for letting Tyler read. He hated Tyler for making a fool out of him. But the worst pain— the knife that really twisted in his guts—was the feeling of betrayal. And Jeremiah was the one who had done that.

When the bell rang for recess, Eric stayed in his seat, dreading the playground. He was surprised to find Peggy Di Angelo beside him.

"C'mon, Eric, let's get some fresh air. This morning was pretty stinky, huh?"

He stood up and walked with her toward the coat-room.

"I sure wouldn't let that Tyler Wayne bug me," she said. Her thin, freckled face was thoughtful. She looked better when she wasn't standing next to someone pretty like Francine.

"I try not to," he agreed.

"He just wants attention, and some kids are dumb enough to give it to him. Not me."

Eric nodded. He didn't know what else to say. They put on their coats and walked down the stairs.

"So what did you do this weekend?" Peggy asked as the cold outside air hit them.

That was almost funny. The greatest weekend of his life, and it was already canceled out. Two hours back in school—*kapow!* Just like that.

"Not much," he said. "How about you?"

"I went out to my aunt's farm. She raises ducks, and they were butchering them. Lots of people ordered ducks for Christmas, so she had to get them all dressed this week. Our whole family helped."

"You have a big family?"

"Two older brothers and a little sister—besides Mom and Dad, of course."

"Lucky."

He tried not to, but he couldn't help watching the group of boys on the far side of the playground. The volunteer hadn't shown up today, so they were just hanging out in a circle, talking. Every time they laughed, Eric wondered if they were talking about him. He looked for Jeremiah in the circle but could not see him.

"Do you know how to skate?" Peggy asked.

"Ice-skate? A little."

"They usually flood the rinks during winter break. You should come down to Pendleton Park. It's the best rink. I always skate there."

"Maybe I will. Say, have you heard anything about

Quatre Cinq being in town?" Eric was surprised to hear himself asking.

"Huh? A famous singer like him here in Mayville? Are you kidding? I'm sure we'd know it if he was."

"Oh, maybe I'm wrong. I saw somebody last night that looked like him."

Peggy just stared at him. Like he was crazy or something. Then she walked over to a bunch of girls. She was probably sorry she had talked to him.

Oh well. Eric stuck his hands in his pockets and toughed it out. By the time recess was over, he was back in control. He knew he could handle it. He'd been stupid to put any faith in Jeremiah. No big deal. He'd just go on as he had before, doing what he had to do. Not expecting anything.

Even the power he thought the black King had given him had been gone when he needed it. Maybe it was only meant for private use. Like helping him when he started missing his dad.

When he got back to the classroom, he was surprised to see Jeremiah in his seat, with his head on his desk. He must not have gone out at all. Eric hesitated. Should he go over to him, perhaps touch his shoulder, ask if he were sick? He stopped himself and turned away. It was probably all an act. Jeremiah just didn't want to face him.

Eric was surprised, too, that Cynthia was *not* in her

seat. He saw that she was near the bookshelves, looking at a dictionary. Remembering that he had not had a chance to leave the new poem on her desk, he hurried to his desk, took it out of his notebook, and headed back toward her desk. Only by that time, Cynthia had finished what she was doing and was making her way carefully back. Eric stopped, hiding the poem behind him. Before he could sneak away, she looked up and saw him.

"Hi. How's it goin', Cynthia?" he said weakly.

Cynthia gave him a fishy look. "*I've* got it together— just like always," she said, but her eyelids lowered when Francine made a deft detour around her without speaking. Eric could see that in spite of her flippant words, being ignored bothered Cynthia just as much as it did him.

He knew he would have to leave the poem for her when she left her desk for lunch; so when the time came, he lagged behind the others, even though he had wanted to be outside early. It was always easier to slip into a group if you were one of the first ones out. But he made up for lost time. Once he was in the lunchroom, he gulped his sandwich, shoved the apple into his pocket, and was one of the first out the door.

"Hey, Stick Boy—are you mad?"

Oh no. Here was Tyler Wayne on his heels, his mouth half full of cookies.

"Who, me?" At least he wasn't answering to that

name. He didn't slow down, either. Just kept walking down the stairs to the outside door.

Tyler stayed right beside him, chewing and smiling his best puppy dog smile. It didn't fool Eric.

"You aren't going to get me in trouble, are you?" Tyler asked. "I didn't mean nothin' by it. Besides, it wasn't my fault. Can I help it if Jerry Peel scribbles like a first-grader?"

Eric opened the door and stepped outside. "Forget it," he said.

Tyler wasn't satisfied. "Well, look. Just tell Miss Arthur I apologized, okay?" He looked nervously over his shoulder. Another bunch of kids was coming out right behind them.

"That was supposed to be 'shogun,' not 'shotgun,' " Eric said.

"D'ya think I'm stupid? Jeez, I saw it on TV." Tyler wiped the cookie crumbs off his mouth and looked again toward the others.

"Then how come you blamed it on the handwriting?" Eric knew his voice was no more than a squeak, but he persisted. For some reason, he was getting to Tyler.

"Well, y'know—that, too. It was just a joke, anyhow."

The door burst open again and a bunch of boys swarmed out. Tyler's crowd. Eric stopped walking.

"I didn't think it was funny," he said softly.

Tyler scowled. "That's because you're such a wimp," he muttered.

"A what?"

Tyler lost his patience. "For Pete's sake, Bonner, are you gonna tell her?"

It flashed across his brain: Tyler had called him by his right name!

"Tell who what?" he persisted.

"Are you gonna tell Miss Arthur that I apologized?"

"I can't. I didn't hear you," Eric said stubbornly.

"All right, then!" Tyler shouted. "I'm sorry I did it. I apologize. *Now* will you tell her?"

There was a sudden silence on the playground. Everyone stood staring at them. Then somebody snickered, and a bunch of others joined in, laughing. Eric knew that this time it was not directed at him.

Tyler's face was red, but he shrugged and turned away from Eric. He reached into his pocket for another cookie and stuffed it into his mouth.

Then Eric heard someone coughing. When he looked over near the front of the school, he saw Jeremiah, shoulders hunched, climbing into Annie's big old car.

Chapter 13

Nothing had changed, really. Still, it had made Eric smile a little when Peggy Di Angelo poked him in the ribs and whispered, "Great strategy!"

The funny thing was, he hadn't been smart at all. He had just lucked out. It wasn't until later that he remembered what Jeremiah had told him about Tyler Wayne's folks whipping him if he ever got in trouble. So Miss Arthur must have threatened to tell Tyler's parents unless he apologized.

He should have known all the time he had Tyler over the barrel. But he hadn't. He had just bumbled his way into forcing the apology in front of all the kids.

Even back in the classroom, he sensed some cautious signals of friendship. Like a new respect. Maybe Tyler wasn't as popular as he appeared to be.

Strangely, that didn't give Eric any pleasure. Even watching Cynthia's slim fingers caressing the wrinkled piece of notebook paper as she read and reread the poem didn't move him at all. And when Francine slipped him a note of apology for thinking he was the one who had told Bonnie Wong about her Secret Friend presents, Eric just nodded to show it was okay. No joy in his heart.

The only thing that really mattered was losing his friend. Whether he was really sick or not, Jeremiah should have given him some sign that they were still friends. Not just friends, but close, sharing friends.

That night Eric telephoned Mr. Robinson.

"Well, hello, Eric. You weren't on the bus today. Was the pageant too much for you yesterday?"

"No, it was great. Thanks for inviting me, Mr. Robinson."

"I was a bit worried about that friend of yours," said Mr. Robinson. "He seemed to have quite a bad cold, and then he got his feet wet, too."

"He had laryngitis today."

"Oh my. Tell him I hope he's better soon."

Sure, Eric thought. Fake laryngitis never lasts long. But he said, "I wasn't on the bus because I had to get a present for my Secret Friend. I walked all the way to Kmart."

"That's a long way. I hope you found what you wanted."

"I *wanted* a Quatre Cinq poster. But we could only spend a dollar. Posters cost a lot more than that."

"Is she a big fan of this . . . uh . . . Quatre person?"

Eric hesitated. He didn't really want to tell Mr. Robinson about the poems.

"Yes, I think she is," he said. "Anyway, I had picked out a pen that writes in three colors; but at the last minute, I saw a spiral notebook with Quatre Cinq on the cover. In color and everything. Just ninety-nine cents."

Mr. Robinson chuckled. "And all that writing paper, too. I guess it was your lucky day."

"Yes and no. How was *your* day?"

"Oh, I went to the senior center. Had a good lunch. Played pinochle. Not as much fun as yesterday, though. Tell your mother I appreciated her driving over."

"I will. Uh . . . I just thought I'd tell you. We get off school at noon Wednesday, so I won't see you on the bus again until after vacation."

"Well, I'll miss you, Eric. But I'm sure you'll be having a good time."

"I don't know. I might call you sometime, if you don't mind."

Of course Mr. Robinson didn't mind. That was the nice thing about him. Even though he never came up with any very good answers, at least he took the time to listen.

After he hung up, Eric found his mother in the bathroom. She was lightening her hair.

"Mr. Robinson says he appreciated your driving yesterday," he said.

Mrs. Bonner grabbed a towel to catch the drips.

"He's a nice person, Eric. Do you suppose he'd like to come over for Christmas dinner on Saturday? If he doesn't have other plans, that is."

"And maybe I could buy him a gift." Eric remembered the wool mittens he had seen in the shop window. They might be marked down by Friday.

He went to his room to wrap Cynthia's gift. One more poem would be nice, but he couldn't think of any. Besides, just the notebook would be enough. He decided not to sign his name. Let her think it was somebody else.

The Kmart bag lay on his bed. He lifted the bottom edge, and the contents spilled out on his bedspread. The package of red tissue paper. The bag of black licorice that he had bought on impulse at the checkout. And the thin spiral notebook with Quatre Cinq staring at him from the cover.

Now that he studied it, he realized he'd been mistaken the other night. The King at the pageant had been darker and had a bigger nose. It was only the eyes that were alike, and the way they moved. Thinking it was Quatre Cinq had been his imagination, after all.

He wrapped the gift in red tissue and taped it shut. It had been the last notebook like that at Kmart. Otherwise, he would have bought one for himself instead of the licorice.

"Eric, aren't you in bed yet? It's nearly ten." His mother must have noticed the light shining under his door.

"I'm just going, Mom."

He took off his shirt. How he hated looking at his long, pale arms. Quickly, he pulled on his pajama top. The sleeves seemed even shorter than usual. It wasn't bad to be tall, but why did he have to be so skinny? Tyler was right. He really *was* a stick boy.

Snapping off the light so he wouldn't have to see himself, Eric crawled under the covers. Then he tore open the licorice and started eating.

Something awful woke him. Like somebody moaning. As his mind cleared, he realized it was himself. When he tried to move, all he could feel was pain. His mouth tasted rotten, and his stomach felt as if it were full of rocks. The room was still pitch-dark, and the glowing red digits on his clock said 4:36.

He started to moan again but forced himself to hold it back. His mom needed her sleep. He dragged his arm across the pillow and heard the crackle of cellophane. The licorice package, nearly empty. Ugh!

What a dummy he was. The very thought of the licorice made his stomach lurch. Eric slipped out of bed and bent over, headed for the bathroom.

His vomit was a disgusting black, and he was still gagging over the toilet bowl when he heard his mother rattling the doorknob. He quickly flushed. He didn't dare let her know he'd eaten all that candy and then thrown up. Knowing her, she'd start worrying he was bulimic.

As it was, she hugged him, felt his face for a temperature, and asked anxious questions.

"Flu, I guess," Eric mumbled. "Going around at school."

"Oh, my poor dear," she soothed. "Maybe it's just too much excitement, with Christmas coming and everything . . ."

"I'll be okay," he said. "I'm going back to bed."

"Yes, get some rest. It's nearly morning, anyway. There'll be no school for you today. If you need anything, call me."

"I'll be fine, Mom. Go back to bed."

Eric stumbled back to his room and fell into bed. Vomiting had helped a little, but not enough. He fumbled for the candy sack and thrust it under his mattress. When he laid his head on the pillow and closed his eyes, he saw weird auras; but as long as he didn't think about licorice, his stomach seemed to behave.

By midmorning he felt much better. The trouble with staying home alone was having all that time to think. Tyler Wayne was probably making up stories about him. Reasons why he wasn't in school. Stuff like that. And Jeremiah would be there, snickering, licking up all Tyler's garbage.

At about eleven-thirty, the phone rang.

"Eric, honey, how are you feeling?"

"I'm better, Mom. I've been up for a while."

"I called school and told them you had stomach flu. The principal hadn't heard of any other cases."

"Oh . . . uh . . . Peggy Di Angelo said her aunt's family had it. They caught it from ducks."

"Ducks?"

"I—I thought she said ducks. Maybe not."

"I think you'd better go back to bed for a while, Eric." His mother sounded quite concerned. "You seem a little feverish. I guess you could take a Tylenol tablet. That might help. Just *one*, though. I'll try to get home as soon as possible after work."

Instead of going back to bed, Eric got dressed. He boiled some water, dropped a bouillon cube in a cup, and had broth for lunch. It felt good in his stomach. Then he watched television all afternoon.

At four o'clock the phone rang, probably his mother again.

He picked it up and heard a lot of coughing.

"Who is this?" he asked suspiciously.

The coughing stopped and a weak voice said, "It's me. Jeremiah. Is this Eric?"

"Yeah." Cold and unfriendly. That's how he wanted to sound. "What do *you* want?"

"I gotta talk to you. I'm in the hospital."

A tremor went down Eric's spine, but he held back,

unwilling to fall for some Tyler Wayne trick. "Quit faking," he said.

Jeremiah coughed again. "It's true. You gotta believe me. I've got pneumonia. Annie took me to the doctor this morning, and he sent me here right away. I think . . . I might be going to die."

Eric was trembling now. Jeremiah's voice was so reedy, so scared. He wasn't a good enough actor to be faking this.

"You're really in the hospital? Jeez, that's too bad."

"Eric, I don't want to die with you being mad at me."

"Die! You won't die. Lots of people get pneumonia. They'll give you something for it."

"I just don't know. The doctors look real serious and go outside the door when they talk."

"C'mon, Jeremiah. You'll be all right. You *will.*"

"Eric, I'm sorry about the report. I was gonna do it, even if my voice wasn't so good; but then Tyler Wayne said . . . he said some stuff, and I—I chickened out. I'm really sorry."

Eric wasn't able to say anything for a minute. What was he supposed to say: That's okay, anytime you want to leave me in the lurch, go right ahead? Let Tyler Wayne call the shots?

"It's easy to say you're sorry, Jeremiah," he said, trying to keep his voice from breaking. "Tyler Wayne even apologized to me yesterday, but what do you think that was worth?"

"I know." Jeremiah's cough sounded more like a sob. "I don't blame you if you hate me, but if I'm gonna die, I just *have* to tell you. I had more fun doing that stuff with you this weekend than I've ever had with anybody. You and your mom were so nice. I felt like I could just be *me* and you liked me, anyway."

"I felt that way too," Eric said quietly.

"But in school it's different. Like it's hard sometimes to be friends with who you want. You know?"

Eric couldn't help thinking of Cynthia Jebber.

"You mean like with a geek—like with a Stick Boy?" he asked, forcing out the words.

"I don't think you're a geek," Jeremiah said.

"Thanks." Eric couldn't hide the bitterness in his voice.

"Eric, I've been trying to think of something I could leave you—if I die, I mean. I haven't got much, but my dad sent me a belt once, with an anchor on the buckle. I never wore it because it's too big. I know it would be big for you, too, but maybe you'll grow into it. Would you like it, Eric?"

Something from Jeremiah's dad? He could hold out against apologies, but this was different. It would be like giving away the wedding picture—his one most prized possession. It had to be for real.

Wet splotches fell on the telephone, and Eric realized he was crying. "Jeremiah, you're going to be all right!" he said, sniffling, trying to keep his voice steady. "You'll be fine, and we'll do some stuff yet during vacation. We're friends, okay?"

So there they sat, on the phone, bawling, until Jeremiah started coughing again and somebody took the phone away from him. Eric was left with a dial tone.

Clouds made the day seem even shorter than usual, and Eric was sitting silently in an almost dark room when he heard footsteps on the stairs. They had to be his mother's, but they sounded different—quick, light, almost skipping. She turned the key and stepped in, switching on the light.

"Oh, Eric," she said, smiling, surprised to see him coming toward her. "I've got something to tell you . . ."

She caught sight of his face and stopped. "What's wrong, Eric? Are you feeling worse?"

"It's Jeremiah," he said. "He's got pneumonia and he's going to die."

She held out her arms, and just like a little kid, he ran to her and sobbed on her shoulder. She hugged him and comforted him, and after a minute he got himself under control.

"It doesn't sound that bad to me," Mrs. Bonner said when Eric had told her about Jeremiah's call. "If he's in the hospital, under treatment, and he's well enough to make phone calls, it just doesn't seem terminal. Was his foster mother there?"

"I don't think so."

"Give me her number. I'll see what I can find out."

A minute later his mom was on the phone with Annie, asking for all the details. She repeated everything Annie said, so Eric could hear.

"Pneumonia? And in both lungs? Oh, he had it before? Yes, a recurrence is risky. But he's on antibiotics now, right? And the doctor says . . . ? Oh, that's great. Then he should be home by Christmas! Just a minute. Eric wants to talk to you, Annie."

"Are you sure he'll be all right?" Eric asked.

"Don't you worry a bit," Annie boomed. "The doc said those antibiotics should do the trick in a couple of days."

"But Jeremiah said—he thought he was going to die. He seemed pretty sure about it."

"Well, he was a pretty sick boy when I first took him to the doc. I got chewed out for not bringing him sooner. Seems he had pneumonia before he came to live with me and didn't think to mention it. Of course, I might not have believed him if he had."

Annie lowered his voice a little. "Jeremiah's a good egg, don't get me wrong. But just between me and you, what Jerry says and the real truth ain't always one and the same. If you know what I mean."

"But he wouldn't lie about a thing like that!"

"I didn't say he lies. Exactly. I know about these messed-up kids—I've took enough of them. And Jerry's one of the best. You got to give him credit, after the way he's been kicked around. Never having a father, and then his mother taking off like that. So sometimes he says what he *needs* to say. See what I mean?"

"I think maybe I do." Eric remembered the German shepherd story.

After he hung up, his mom put her arm around him again. "Do you feel better now?" she asked.

He nodded. He could smell her LeJardin cologne.

"In that case, listen to this," she said, her eyes shining. "Old Waldo came in this afternoon and handed me a two-hundred-dollar Christmas bonus. Plus, he's giving me two extra days off and a raise beginning the first of the year!"

"Wow!"

"What do you say I call that Chinese place and have them deliver some cashew chicken?"

"My favorite," said Eric. He could hardly believe his daydream was coming true. Just the way he'd imagined it on the bus. Maybe he had something in common with that guy Isaiah in the Bible, after all.

Chapter 14

Eric's mother drove him to school on Wednesday morning. Not because he was still sick. He was fine, except for a few strange tingles when he thought about what had been happening in the past couple of days. He was still feeling confused about a few things.

The reason for the ride to school was that he had so much to carry. Besides Cynthia's present (concealed in a brown paper bag), he had a big Tupperware tray full of raw vegetables. The school was only furnishing hot dogs, so Eric was not surprised that his mom made him bring something nutritious.

She had also handed him a get-well card.

"Have all the kids sign it, and we'll take it to Jeremiah at the hospital tonight," she said. "Won't he like that?"

Eric knew he would.

The first thing he did after taking his vegetables to the lunchroom was to give the card to Miss Arthur. It was not what he wanted to do at all. He really wanted to stride around the room, waving the card.

"Here, sign this! It's for my friend Jeremiah. He *is* my friend—my very best friend, you know."

But of course he couldn't do that. Letting everyone know they were friends had to be Jeremiah's decision. He could see that now.

That was one thing Jeremiah had been very truthful about, and Annie's phone call had helped Eric to understand, too. Even though it hurt to admit it, he knew that Jeremiah might have to pay a price for their friendship.

So he would let Miss Arthur ask for the signatures and then quietly pick up the card later.

Everybody seemed in a good mood. For almost an hour they sang Christmas carols, led by Miss Arthur's enthusiastic piano playing. Then she pulled the drapes for a special treat. She had borrowed a projector and the film *Miracle on Thirty-fourth Street.*

After the film came the gift exchange. Eric hardly looked at the small package he was given. He found an excuse to be up in front when Cynthia tore the red tissue paper off his gift. He watched her face crinkle into a happy smile when she saw the notebook with Quatre Cinq on the cover. She flipped the wrapper over a few times, looking for a name tag. Then she turned around, looking up and down the rows, as if trying to figure out who it could be from.

Maybe he should have put his name on it after all. He supposed he was a coward not to. He glanced at his own package and ripped off the wrapping. It was a blank cassette tape. And the card inside was signed "Jeremiah Peel."

"So, did Jerry Peel get you a nice present?" Tyler Wayne's mocking voice was right behind Eric.

How did he know? Too late, Eric tried to pretend indifference, but he knew Tyler had seen the surprised look on his face.

"Oh, yeah, Stick Boy"—the room was so noisy Tyler dared to use the name—"bet you didn't know Peel had your name, huh? Well, he *didn't*, until the other day when I gave him fifty cents to take it off *my* hands. Sorry about that!" Tyler almost doubled over with laughter.

Again Eric shriveled inside. No matter which way he turned, Tyler Wayne was one step ahead, waiting to hurt him. Someday, he thought, you're going to get what you deserve.

But of course the day was spoiled again. It always was. He couldn't even get too excited when Miss Arthur called them into the lunchroom. She must have slipped out during the movie to decorate. The two food tables were on the side by the windows, and she had put wreaths and silver stars on colored ribbons in all the windows. The lunch tables were not pushed together in the usual long rows, either, but were individually arranged, each with a white paper covering.

The hot dogs were steaming in a Nesco, and everyone got in line to start filling their paper plates. As usual, Eric chose a table in the back, while Tyler Wayne grabbed one for his friends as close to the food as possible.

Cynthia was having some trouble with her braces, and Miss Arthur helped her to fill her plate. Then Miss Arthur found a place for Cynthia to sit and sat down at that table herself, chatting with all the kids.

There were some empty spaces at Eric's table, and he was surprised when the two boys who had teased him about the food fight sat next to him, acting really friendly.

He had almost cleaned his plate when Miss Arthur jumped to her feet and started rearranging things on the front tables.

"Will a couple of you set the salads back and put the desserts in front now?" she asked. "And Richard, would you help me carry these leftover hot dogs down to the gym? The younger kids are eating down there and might need extras."

Together she and Richard Johnson left the room, carrying the big Nesco roaster. Francine and Peggy hurried to take the covers off the desserts and move them forward.

"Oh, look at this!"

"Aren't those scrumptious?"

Everyone was exclaiming about the assortment of decorated cookies; pink and white popcorn balls; nut cups; pink lemonade; and, prettiest of all, a huge flat box filled with two dozen double-decker cupcakes, all covered with fluffy white frosting and coconut, decorated to look like snowmen. Each had little chocolate-chip buttons and eyes, and a tiny sliver of red gumdrop smile.

Tyler Wayne was the first one to grab. He filled his plate with goodies and then picked up one of the snowman cupcakes, biting into it as he walked back to his table. It was chocolate inside, and he smacked his lips.

The other kids had slightly better manners, lining up for their desserts and lemonade. Eric stayed at his table. He could wait until the big rush was over. The snowmen were going fast, but there were only twenty kids in the room—he knew there would be enough.

Francine was waltzing back to her table, carrying a snowman cupcake. "Isn't this just adorable?" she exclaimed. "Who brought these, anyway?"

"I did," Cynthia said shyly. "I made them myself."

Francine froze in her tracks. Voices stopped. Breathing stopped. Francine's eyes, in a face that was no longer so pretty, sent out a silent call for help. Nobody answered. She quickly slipped into her chair and set the cupcake on the table, far from her plate.

At his table near the desserts, Tyler Wayne's face had turned a deep red. In front of him sat his snowman, already half eaten.

"Ugh," he grunted. "I ain't eating that garbage." He stood, picked up the snowman, took a few steps, and tossed it into a wastebasket.

One by one, those who were eating cupcakes set them down. On all the tables sat snowman cupcakes, some with dark bite marks—all suddenly rejected.

Those who had been in line quickly picked up a few cookies and sat down, eyes lowered. Nobody dared to look at Cynthia.

Eric sat frozen. *Do something, somebody!* he wanted to scream, but no words came. He wasn't surprised at Tyler, but how could Francine have done a thing like that? He looked at Peggy Di Angelo. She looked pale and worried, fidgeting in her chair; but her snowman was pushed to the side of her plate, too. Where was the fair leader they needed?

And then Eric saw the look on Cynthia's face. Gone was the joy of seeing the Quatre Cinq cover, the pride of bringing the best dessert. There was such terrible anguish in her face that he had to close his eyes.

For a second he tried his old trick, focusing on the

texture of the white table cover, blotting out what he could not bear to see. But that didn't work, and suddenly he knew. This time he had to use the King's gift. He had to *be* the King of Orient—a leader sure to be fair.

His vision blurred and an unseen force lifted him to his feet until he stood majestically in shimmering costume. He could almost feel a jeweled crown pressing against his forehead. As in a dream, he was aware of the shining blackness of his face; he was confident, powerful as he walked straight up the full length of the lunchroom.

He walked past Francine, and past Peggy Di Angelo, and past all the others who were doing nothing to help. The King walked slowly and steadily even though he knew everyone was looking at him. He stopped in front of the flat box and slowly stretched one skinny arm so everyone could see, and picked the biggest, fattest snowman of all.

The black King turned toward the sixth grade and took a very large bite of snowman. He savored it, and then moved over to the table where Cynthia sat. She was staring down at her plate, her face like dark, chiseled stone.

The black King spoke in the voice Eric remembered so well. It was a quiet voice, but it held authority. It held peace.

"Thank you for bringing the cupcakes, Cynthia. This is the best cupcake I have ever eaten."

He could hear Peggy Di Angelo's voice then. "I love

this snowman, too, Cynthia!" she yelled. Eric knew he had given her courage to speak. And others followed the leader until there was a small chorus of voices. "So do I. Me, too."

Suddenly, Cynthia's head jerked up, and she was glaring at Eric. "Don't do me any favors, Eric Bonner!" she yelled.

He stepped back, amazed, as she struggled to her feet, grabbed for her cane, and limped across to the wastebasket. She reached down and pulled out the mangled remains of Tyler Wayne's snowman. Without a second's warning, she flung it straight into Tyler's face. He let out a roar, but she was already turning away.

"From now on, I'll fight my own battles," she lashed out again at Eric.

Shocked by her attack, he started to tremble. He was Eric Bonner again, forgetting about his royal presence.

"I'm sorry," he mumbled.

"I guess you all think I don't have feelings," Cynthia said, stamping her cane. Everyone seemed too stunned to answer, but she went on. "Well, I do. And it's not too nice when nobody talks to you, and nobody sits by you. There's only one person in this school who knows anything about me. That's my Secret Friend, and I don't even know who she is. As for you, Eric Bonner, I hope you and everybody else in this nice Christian school go straight to hell."

Still speechless, Eric glanced around the room. Tyler

Wayne was silently dabbing at his face with a napkin. He looked numb with shock.

The whole sixth grade just sat there—totally freaked out. Who would have expected a thing like this to happen?

One shaky voice said, "We're sorry, Cynthia." It sounded like Peggy Di Angelo. There were some other sympathetic murmurs.

But there was too much tension in the air for peacemaking, and Eric realized something had to be done. He wished desperately that Jeremiah were here to help him. But he knew that sometimes you have to go it alone.

What was needed was an epilogue—one more scene to be played out.

The black King of Orient (or was it really Quatre Cinq?) pushed Eric aside and sprang back into character. He looked Cynthia squarely in her angry face.

"Cynthia Jebber," he said, slowly and deliberately. "There's something you need to know." Raising his fingers in a jaunty four-five salute, his feet moved into a Quatre Cinq routine—shaky but recognizable—and he half sang, half whispered the words: " 'That sinking feeling / turning upside down / walking on my hands / into Spidertown.' "

Cynthia's eyes widened and her mouth fell open. A whole assortment of expressions crossed her face, until she finally understood. "You!" she gasped. "Quatre Cinq, my Secret Friend?"

"I will be, if you'll let me," he said. He was Eric again, but this time the power was still sticking with him.

He spun around on his heel. "Keep travelin', man/ till you find your niche!" he croaked.

Then he began to laugh, and Cynthia laughed, and that whole crazy classroom of copycats started laughing too. Honest, friendly, relieved laughter. And once they had started, it was impossible to stop.